THE STAR OF SUTHERLAND

GENE BREAZNELL

Walker & Co.
New York

Copyright © 1990 by Gene Breaznell
All rights reserved. No part of this book may be reproduced or
transmitted in any form or by any means, electronic or mechanical,
including photocopying, recording, or by any information storage and
retrieval system, without permission in writing of the Publisher.
All the characters and events portrayed in this work are fictitious.
First published in the United States of America in 1990
by Walker Publishing Company, Inc.
Published simultaneously in Canada by Thomas Allen & Son
Canada, Limited, Markham, Ontario
Library of Congress Cataloging-in-Publication Data
Gene Breaznell
The Star of Sutherland / Gene Breaznell
ISBN 0-8027-5754-5
I. Title.
PS3552.R3577S7   1990
813'.54—dc20   89-48087
CIP

Printed in the United States of America
2 4 6 8 10 9 7 5 3 1

THE STAR OF SUTHERLAND

For Annie

Prologue

Last September, a South Carolina redneck working on a road crew found the largest diamond ever discovered in the United States, and one of the largest in the world. There are diamonds in the South, and it once had a producing diamond mine. But don't rush off to South Carolina to look for another "Star of Sutherland." The odds of finding a diamond that size are a billion to one, and it cost Cowpens Martin, the redneck who found it, his life.

▽

Chapter 1

THE FIRST TIME I saw Cowpens Martin, he lay under a pinball machine. He wasn't dead, just dead drunk, hugging the spit and sawdust floor of Elmer's Tradewinds Lounge in Sutherland, South Carolina. The machine above him rattled along at the hands of a Sutherland College student whose friends stood around him watching, swilling Blue Ribbon beer, entranced by the silver ball skating through trippers, flippers, and multicolored lights, oblivious to the poor little drunk lying just beneath them.

"Damn!" the player cursed as the machine pumped out the numbers of his total score and callously indicated the game was over. "Don't even get a replay," he drawled.

His friends laughed and he indignantly stepped away from the machine and noticed, as if for the first time, Cowpens Martin below. Ignoring gibes that ridiculed his pinball artistry, he ceremoniously hawked up a large amount of expectorant and spat down.

"Gross!" someone squealed.

"Right on his cheek," said another.

"Anybody down there?" asked the spitter in mock concern.

The laughter stopped and all attention turned to Cowpens Martin.

1

"Hell, no, ain't nobody down there, 'less you count some old sleep-it-off redneck."

They laughed again as the boy's phlegm dribbled down Cowpens's beard-stubbled cheek. The other boys spat on him and someone stomped on his ratty, sweat-stained straw Stetson that lay nearby. Kids can be cruel, and those were. It seemed they held more respect for the mindless pinball machine, which could at least protect itself by crying *Tilt*, than for the helpless little man on the floor, whom I was to find kindness would not have been lost on. That night, however, Cowpens Martin was just another town drunk to me. If he had a job, I didn't know. If he had a home, it must have been under that pinball machine.

My eyes retreated to the matte black walls of the dimly lit Elmer's Tradewinds Lounge. I was sure that all the darkness was meant to be seductive, but Elmer, the bar's owner and proprietor, had also hung signs and posters all over the place that were garishly painted in luminescent orange, and made his lounge look like a busy black velvet painting. The Tradewinds Lounge was a redneck's idea of what a college bar should be. The music from the jukebox was loud but there was no country-and-western. Elmer had gotten that right, but the success of the lounge came more from its proximity to Sutherland College than from his poor attempts to achieve something other than the standard, ubiquitous Southern workingman's bar. And Elmer's obsequiousness to the college crowd amused me. His fellow rednecks were not welcome, and were often thrown out or barred at the door. I wondered why Cowpens Martin, the lowliest of rednecks, was allowed to clutter even the small space under the pinball machine. . . .

"What's yours, pardner?" Elmer stuck his flattop haircut and big nose under the glow of a revolving Schlitz globe that dangled from the ceiling near my place at the bar.

"Huh? . . . Oh, a bottle of Bud, please," I replied mechanically, again absorbed in the cruel hazing of Cowpens Martin by the college-bred beer drinkers.

"Bottle of Bud." Elmer gaily bubbled the *B*'s in the phrase, the way Bing Crosby would. "Say that fast and it sounds like a fart in a bathtub, don't it, pardner?" He bent to the refrigerator and withdrew a long-necked brown bottle.

"Bottle of Bud." I said it fast and smiled faintly, trying to catch Elmer's onomatopoeia.

"Right, pardner." Elmer laughed and popped the cap off the bottle, releasing an effervescent hiss not half as sweet and pungent as flatus released from the depths of a warm bath, and flat compared with Bing Crosby's oval *B*'s. He set the bottle before me and went away, clearing empties from the bar and smashing them into big plastic tubs.

I sipped the beer and continued to peruse the relatively empty Tradewinds Lounge. Three coeds sat at a table in a dark corner and talked intently among themselves, paying no attention to the pinball wizards still surrounding Cowpens Martin. Two more unescorted girls entered but I ignored them. I was too far past the college crowd . . . oh, not so far that I couldn't put the moves on a college girl, for at thirty-eight I still looked pretty young and might even have passed for a perpetual college senior. No, I was too far removed to be motivated, for in a few days I would be the English professor for some of those kids and I had to remain somewhat aloof.

Also, I must admit, I didn't have the heart to try to make it with any young things. I had just come back to Sutherland College, my alma mater. I had fled the Northeast, Saratoga Springs, New York, where I had been teaching college English, when my wife had left me and taken our year-old child.

I did not know where she was and I didn't care. Of course I cared about my little daughter, but I was severely distressed and depressed that my wife could leave me for a horse trainer—an uneducated, galloping growth of gaucherie, I thought, although I'd never seen him. Her timing was good, though. She left me at the end of summer recess, so I had all of two weeks to figure out what to do with my life. I was scheduled to go on teaching in Saratoga Springs, but I couldn't bring myself to stay at the scene of the crime, to face all of the memories and the gossip. So I rationalized that my untenured teaching job had always been tenuous and I left. I didn't feel I'd screwed the college, for there are always a hundred other English professors just waiting to be plugged in at a moment's notice. I know. That's how I was plugged in at Sutherland College.

If you don't know what it's like to cancel one life and start completely over, I can tell you. First, you throw out everything you have, everything that isn't absolutely necessary, anything that won't fit conveniently into your car. Books, records, and magazines are out because they weigh too much, and furniture is of course a no-no. Extra clothes are out too, as are most sports equipment, kitchen utensils, full sets of Nine Flags cologne, and any geegaws that could slow you down or make your car use too much gas. You can keep your toothbrush and your tennis racquet, but you'd better give up golf.

After I had eliminated all the excess, all the "good stuff" that everybody thinks they desperately need but that they wouldn't miss for a moment if it suddenly disappeared, I hopped into my car and drove south. Going that direction has its advantages, like letting you leave behind bulky, space-wasting overcoats and the miserable reticulum of Northeast toll roads. I must say I didn't consider those advantages at the time, and I certainly didn't consider stopping in Sutherland, South Carolina. I'd had enough of college life and I was headed for Florida, the "Land of Fresh Starts," according to some blurb I'd once read from The Sunshine State's chamber of commerce. I was lucky that my wife had run away in the horse trainer's car (with that kind of luck I stay away from racetracks), because she had left me with my aged but reliable Pontiac Tempest. I was pretty sure that old clunker could make it to Florida, but I don't think I even cared when I first aimed myself down the New York State Thruway.

Soon, though, it became a relief to be on the road, slightly numb but suddenly detached from all responsibility. My Tempest purred and the tempest in my soul was being purged for the moment. The air whistled through the vent window, which had never shut completely since the car was new, and serenaded me along with the humming tires, the comfortably burbling exhaust note and the "Dew-Wop" sound from an oldies station that droned low on the Tempest's tinny radio. The sun glowed through the windshield, highlighting the dust on the dashboard and outlining my daughter's little finger smudges on the glass. It didn't bother me, though. I just reached into the glove compartment and wiped everything away with a rag I used to check the oil.

It was that simple. Until dark. It's sunset that triggers man's homing instinct. I believe it goes back to the caveman, who had to duck inside by the fire or be eaten by night-prowling monsters. And there was my problem. I suddenly realized, as the sun disappeared off to my right in the wilds of New Jersey, that I had no place to duck into. No hearth. No warmth. No welcome. I had only Interstate 95, only a big flat concrete snake that would, if I wished, permit me to run up and down the Eastern Seaboard forever. So, after two days of driving and a night of abject drunken loneliness in a cheap motel, I veered off of Interstate 95, and angled westward on Interstate 85 toward Sutherland, South Carolina. I hoped I'd make some contacts from my undergraduate days there, and perhaps see some friendly faces. Maybe I'd find work. . . .

"'Nother Bud, pardner?" Elmer interrupted my reverie, unmindful that I so seriously pondered my empty life, but keenly aware of my empty bottle.

"Sure." I consented so he'd leave me alone for as long as it would take to kill another brew, and so I could drown the thoughts of my wife with that horse trainer.

I hate horses. Say what you will, but I've never deemed horse racing the sport of kings. I'm no snob, but I've seen the compulsive gamblers, touts, panhandlers, and washouts who frequent the tracks, even the most fashionable ones like Saratoga. If they're kings, they rule in hell. Gambling is hell as far as I'm concerned and, though I'm seldom so beleagueringly moral, I'm sure that even the poor horse deserves better than its handlers, handicappers, and what have you. Anyway, I hoped that horse trainer was handling my wife better than I did. Maybe he deserved her. She was a nag. . . .

I felt Elmer's presence again, stalking me, checking my progress with the suds. He leaned under the Schlitz globe, in a posture that was becoming all too familiar, but my attention was suddenly diverted to more disturbance by the pinball machine. Cowpens Martin had stirred, snorted, turned onto his back and, still unconscious, had kicked the machine and sent it on tilt.

"Let's take his boots," someone said, and two boys reached down and wrestled Cowpens's battered and scuffed cowboy boots from his skinny legs, revealing white socks that were stained brown from unbreathing leather, and craggy toes that poked through holes in the stinking socks. His obscene yellow toenails seemed never to have been trimmed.

"They're just funnin'," Elmer chuckled, noticing that my attention was riveted to the scene, and that I'd stopped drinking.

"It doesn't look like fun." I felt further removed from the college kids than ever.

"They like old Cowpens," Elmer insisted. "They're gonna give them boots back too, 'specially when they get a whiff of them socks."

"If they like him, why do they spit on him?" I was annoyed that Elmer condoned the "fun" and that his toadyism for the sake of the college kids' business blinded him to the cruel abuse of a person of his own ilk. Certainly these kids thought little more of that cracker, Elmer, than they did of Cowpens Martin.

"Forget it, pardner. Have another beer."

I spurned Elmer's pitch—I wouldn't have taken another beer for free—and walked out of the Tradewinds Lounge.

Outside, the night air was warm and pleasant but I was more impressed by the quiet and the lack of traffic in that section of Sutherland, and in the whole city for that matter. Saratoga Springs always seemed bustling, especially in the summer with the racing season and the ballet. It's not that Sutherland was dead. It just seemed to be resting. It was only eleven o'clock but the town had gone to bed already, before the late news and the *Johnny Carson Show*. I was sure that nobody in Sutherland had ever seen Johnny's slick little monologue, his sly grins and innuendo, and I was just as sure that nobody cared. I walked to my car in the eerie silence and chuckled to think that the hit talk shows in Sutherland, South Carolina, must be the five a.m. *Farmer's Report*, where the monologue consisted of some old sodbuster's

advice on when to spray for boll weevils; and *The Jerry
Falwell Show*, where innuendo was not even breathed.

I got in my car and drove to the 7/Eleven, where I bought
a six-pack of beer to nurse back at the Peachblossom Motel.
I had been staying there the past few days but I was running
out of money. My wife had taken our entire savings account,
and I would have to look for a rooming house in the morning.

At the Peachblossom, I lay on my bed and drank while
the television reran an ancient Porter Wagoner show, a
country music show that featured Dolly Parton and was
produced before Dolly was cantilevered to super-stardom.
That show led into the late news, local happenings in the
Piedmont area of South Carolina.

In case you don't know, the Piedmont is a rolling land-
mass that runs from the Blue Ridge Mountains to the
Carolina coastal plain. Sutherland is on the Piedmont, near
the foothills of the Blue Ridge Mountains—the wall of rock
that had long ago been uplifted from a crack in the great
tectonic plate that forms North America. As rivers, streams,
and weather carved that wall of stone into the mountains
that are there today, the Piedmont was worn level. Then, in
more recent geologic time, with the elements continually
attacking, the old flattened Piedmont surface was worn some
more. V-shaped valleys were cut into it, forming the youthful
appearing topography that exists today. Those valleys can
fool the undiscerning eye into thinking the Piedmont is
young, but it is very, very old. "Youth imposed upon old age,"
my geology professor had called it as he drove home the
lesson that what you see is not always what you get. He also
told us to beware of the kudzu vine, the rampaging, all-
smothering blanket of chlorophyll that covers the Southern
states and hides clues to the earth's development.

I paid little attention to the late news as my mind wandered through memorable lessons of my undergraduate days. Through my reminiscing, and through my beery haze, I did hear the television news announcer say something about a nonevent in the town of Tryon, North Carolina. Tryon was in the Blue Ridge Mountains not far from Sutherland, and it was good horse country, I unfortunately recollected. Then I smiled as I thought of the old joke about Sutherland College students taking their dates to Tryon, to try them on. That joke would be pretty tame now, but it was very risque for the South when I first went there as a college freshman. I thought about my old college town. I'd barely had a chance to reexplore Sutherland since arriving only a few days ago, but I had noticed that the only youth imposed upon old age there was the college students returning for the fall term. It was readily evident that Sutherland had changed little in the sixteen years since I'd been there, years that had seen cataclysmic evolvement for me.

My name, by the way, is Jim Harrington. I wasn't sure I'd tell it. In fact, I wasn't sure I'd even tell the story of The Star of Sutherland. For I was as guilty as anyone and, in my selfishness and greed, I was probably as thoughtless and as cruel as anyone toward the poor little redneck, Cowpens Martin. But there it is: plain Jim Harrington. I never had a nickname. Sure, sometimes somebody called me Jimmy, but I guess I was a serious kid. And I had no physical irregularities that would cause me to be called four eyes or fatso. I'm of average height, if five-feet-nine inches is average anymore in the shadow of the new generation of behemoths I have absurdly called college kids. I've never been what you'd call good looking, but I have tried to keep in shape; running and watching my diet, except for my weakness, which is ice cream. I'm sure the cold, smooth stuff has done more than clog my arteries. I'm sure it caused my wife to split with the horse trainer, since my raids to the refrigerator for a pint far outnumbered my forays beneath the sheets. Moral: don't abandon your marital duty for tutti-frutti. I saw it as I killed my six-pack in the sickly light of television test patterns, as Sutherland stagnated in the Piedmont and waited for dawn. And I still hate horses.

In the morning, my head hurt. The Peachblossom's checkout time was noon, but I did it at nine so I could get some breakfast and be on my way to find a rooming house. Over eggs and grits in the Peachblossom's dilapidated dining room, I looked for rooming houses in *The Sutherland Herald*, a wafer-thin mullet wrapper with hardly enough rag content to stay together for swatting the Peachblossom's plethora of flies. I skimmed past the society section, where I noticed the big news was Bessie Boatwright's engagement party: punch was served from a crystal bowl. When I got to the classifieds, one ad leapt out at me: *Room For Rent, $20 per wk, maid ser, Hugh Carswell, 22 Magnolia St*. I wondered how a decent room could be only twenty dollars per week, with maid service to boot. My motel room had cost that much per night, and the Peachblossom didn't smell like one. But my wallet was thinner than *The Sutherland Herald*, and the Peach-blossom's grits, so I decided to ride by 22 Magnolia.

To my surprise, Magnolia Street turned out to be a gorgeous cul-de-sac in one of Sutherland's prettiest old sections. Knowing little about architecture, and having just escaped from the ornate Victoriana of Saratoga Springs, the houses on Magnolia Street were what I termed "Southern Simple." They were solid, well-kept frame houses, each surrounded by lush, trimmed foliage, some boasting giant, elegant trees of the genus the street was named after. Still, I expected the worst as I cruised toward number twenty-two.

My fears were unfounded. Hugh Carswell's house seemed to match the others in pleasing ambiance. It was big and white and looked recently painted. It was also larger than most of the other houses and, as my Tempest slowed to a crawl, I spied a side entrance that I hoped was a private one to the room for rent. I parked in front of the house and opened my door very slowly so the usual rasping squeal of the long-rusted hinges would not defile the genteel old neighborhood. I walked to Hugh Carswell's front door and found that it was open but screened. The huge front porch was as vacant and tidy as a ship's deck, and just as thick with layers of gray paint. I pressed the doorbell and immediately sensed a stirring somewhere deep inside the old house. Then I heard steps that grudgingly plodded closer, accompanied by mumbles of complaint at having to make the trek to the front door. A young black woman in a white maid's uniform appeared. Through the screen she looked sleek, lithe, and muscular, like a sprinter—as if she could beat Evelyn Ashford in the hundred and shouldn't have had such a struggle to get from one side of the house to the other.

"Mr. Carswell in?" I asked.

"Ain't no Mistah Carswell," she sang through the screen and disappeared back into the house before I could speak again.

I didn't feel I'd been dismissed, so I stayed and peered into the living room. It looked clean, with solid, simple furniture to match the Southern Simple facade of the house. Stubby fringed-shade lamps squatted on thick round tables. There was a plush sofa and there were overstuffed chairs with starched white doilies on every arm and back. If the room for rent was anything like the living room, I'd surely take it. From nowhere, an old lady in a baggy house dress and slippers appeared at the front door.

"Ah'm Mrs. Carswell," she said. "Y'all lookin' for a room?"

"Well, there's just me," I said looking behind me, but she failed to get my little joke. "Yes, ma'am," I quickly added, not wanting to put her off, recalling that the Southern psyche demanded politeness.

"You with the college?" The old lady looked distrustful.

"Yes, ma'am," I said simply, giving her time to appraise me, acting as though I had all morning for an interview.

"You mighta come to the right place." She squinted and, looking for God knows what little old ladies look for when confronted by a stranger, she finally gave me a smile of acceptance that showed her lack of upper front teeth. She slipped an arthritic hand into a big pocket in her house dress, unlatched the screen door, and handed me a key.

"Have a look," she said. "Walk up the stairs around to the side. It'll be the first door to your right, past the kitchen and bathroom."

"Yes, ma'am." This time my answer was stilted, meant to be noncommittal. I had no idea what to expect upstairs.

"You don't drink and party, now, do you?" Her words held me as I turned to go to the room.

"No, ma'am," I replied, feeling that "yes, ma'am" and "no, ma'am" were all that were needed to communicate in the South, but adding, "I don't even smoke."

"That's nice." She nodded, looked to the heavens and ethereally closed her eyes.

I walked around to the side of the house, past a row of thick azaleas that must have been a bombardment of color in the spring, and entered the side door. I climbed the stairs to the second story and found myself in a small kitchen. A hallway ran to the left and to the right, and down each side of the hall were closed doors that probably led to the rooms of the other tenants. From the kitchen, I turned right and passed the open door to the communal bathroom. I'm not overly fussy, but it looked very clean and I was pleased. Past the bath, I unlocked the first door on the right and entered a small room, a pleasant rectangle painted light blue, with a mirror-faced armoire, a good-sized dresser with a large mirror above it, and a comfortable looking bed with a mahogany headboard. It was a corner room and its two big windows were wide open to a warm September breeze that reminded me it could be as hot as hell in South Carolina through that month. I looked at myself in one of the mirrors. I needed a shave and I had circles under my eyes from wrestling with memories and my six-pack until dawn. The room was fine and I was ready to occupy the bed. Since I had not seen or heard anyone on that floor, I assumed that the other tenants were respectable working people like myself. I went back down to Mrs. Carswell, took the room and, before unpacking my car, went back up for a nap.

I stripped in front of the mirrored armoire and stared at my naked body. I hadn't taken a good look at myself in a while. I'd lost weight and I liked it. In the trauma of losing my wife and child, I had switched from ice cream to beer, ignoring food and drinking until I puked. It was a strange paradox that my body looked so defined and fit, that physical and mental abuse had made my abdominal muscles show and had chiseled my physique. I flexed a muscle here and there and, for the first time in weeks, felt that all was not lost. I felt that, although my mind had temporarily succumbed to my misery, my body had sustained the spark necessary for recovery. I crooked my left arm, bunching the bicep, and saw elasticity.

Don't get me wrong, I'm no narcissistic muscle pumper. In fact, I wanted to keep as far away from the guy in the

mirror as I could. I knew there were better lovers than my
left hand, though I confess I've never been ashamed to use
that solicitous southpaw stroker when the chips were down.
But this time, as I scanned my image, my penis stayed small.
It had taken second priority to the rest of my body. Oh, I
liked my organ, don't misunderstand, but it seemed unob-
trusive in the scheme of things, very undemanding and
hardly the center of my being. Sex could wait. There seemed
no point to it when the only fantasy that filled my mind was
a vision of my wife with that horse trainer. I wondered if he
was hung like a horse and admit that I, Jim Harrington of
no nickname, had sometimes fantasized about being called
"Big Jimbo," or "Dirigible Dick," or "Gas Pump"—something befitting the "high bankers" a Southern college chum
had once described, who proudly displayed their prodigious,
semierect appendages high on the banks of the old swim-
ming hole while lesser-hung, ashamedly shriveled mere
mortals stripped and quickly slipped into the water. . . .

I slept. There was no time. Just a long, leaden, dreamless
clot in the Southern-hot onset of my rematriculation to
Sutherland and its college. When I finally awoke, it was dark
and I was hungry. for the first time in a long time I was
anxious for food instead of alcohol. I felt I could eat at a place
that didn't serve beer, and I hoped it wasn't too late to find
one. I found the light switch and also found that my watch
had stopped. I craved a chili cheeseburger from a drive-in
that was nearby, but that closed at midnight. I hurried into
my clothes and rushed out of my room. The light was on in
the kitchen and a man sat at the table with his back to me.

"Excuse me, sir, do you have the time?" I exuded Southern
politeness, hoping to be rewarded with the knowledge that
I had time to make it to the drive-in.

The man looked at his wrist and turned so I could see his faded, flowered, Western-style shirt with fancy basting and pearl snaps.

"Shore do," he announced in a turnip-green twang. "It's lebin-tin. How're y'all?"

It was Cowpens Martin.

▽

Chapter 2

FRESH FACES, FRESHMAN ENGLISH. Pencils poised, minds on the alert. It would pass. The doldrums of a long semester would see to it. The men would stop shaving, and the women setting their hair, and they'd show up in sweatshirts and cutoffs. Fraternity and sorority rushes, with the constant drinking and dope, would take their toll, and then they'd remember how to yawn. Then I'd have to stand on my head, naked, to get their attention, and even that wouldn't last very long. At the semester's start, however, every polished face in the sea of abysmal ignorance before me hung on my every word and sedulously recorded my more salient points in their shiny new notebooks.

I'd pass them all. They only had to attend most of the classes. Show up and get a *D* was my motto. If they failed, I had failed to make it interesting and challenging. Still, I'd never be able to reach some of them, and it wouldn't affect me. I was well aware that freshman English was a required course, and that I couldn't force math majors and physicists, orderly minded methodologists, to love the obscure conceits of the metaphysical poets. I couldn't sell Donne door-to-door. Nor would I try to shove the beatitudes of Browning, Byron, and Barchester Towers down their throats. I recalled all too well the required religion courses at Sutherland College, before Yates Sutherland took over from his father as college president. Though the Sutherland family owned every cotton mill in that part of South Carolina, the college was founded on Methodist principles, Methodist endowments, and church-related tax shelters. Thus, religion was a required freshman course until Yates made it elective: the Methodist Church needn't have worried, for Sutherland College still had its share of preministerial students who emerged every year like excess flab bulging over the confines of the Bible Belt.

As freshmen, Yates and I were in the same required religion class. He slept, like so many others, while our white-haired professor read from the Bible through steel-rimmed glasses as though we hung on every word. The old man preached and proselytized, and turned his lectern into a pulpit. His word was absolute gospel, his mind too inagile to guide bored students through the Biblical melodrama and tell them who Jesus Christ really was. Thank God, and Yates Sutherland, that those soporific sermons had been replaced by courses in the philosophy of religion, relieving young minds that would rather pulverize the sacred shrouds for scrutiny under an electron microscope of the ecclesiastical fairy tales.

Yes, it was a good thing that Yates Sutherland had fallen asleep. And I would not put my English classes to sleep. I'd have them look at the classics in a different light. I'd show them Beowulf from the view of the mead hall-menacing monster instead of the good guy, ala John Gardner. I'd guide them carefully through the chubby tome labeled *Norton's Anthology* so they wouldn't have to suffer every page and the copious footnotes, so their delicate hands wouldn't get paper cut and infected with that dread French disease, "tome-main poisoning."

Thus armed, and ready to draw instantly from my arsenal of bad puns, a hot-shit, liberal, carpetbagging English teacher looked over his class on that first day and called the roll. I recognized two of the students who had tormented Cowpens Martin under the pinball machine at Elmer's Tradewinds Lounge. One had helped take his boots and the other was the spitter. I wondered if they would cause mischief in class, but I quickly forgot them as I continued the roll, stumbling on some names and savoring the Southern ones: Loquita Scruggs, Elrod Cheatham, Capers Smith, Stiles Harper, Petulia Smithyman, Doyle Swofford, Joab Lesesne, Bates Scoggins. . . . I asked them all where they were from. Most were from the South, some from jerkwater, one-stoplight burgs, and some from bigger towns like Ninety-six, Gaffney, Due West, Walhalla, Roebuck, Eutawville, Pacolet, and Chesnee. Some sniggered at those from the tiny towns, for they hailed from Columbia, Savannah, Charlotte, or— hold your breath—the megalopolis of Atlanta, the New York City of The New South: mushmouth mecca. All roads lead to Atlanta and, if you've ever been in that airport, all the air routes in the country, too.

I could tell the football players; they had no necks and their thighs were as big around as my waist. For some reason, they sat bunched like a flying wedge at the back of the room. Occasionally they huddled to discuss something I had said, or to evaluate one of the coeds. Anyway, I liked them. They laughed the loudest and, I thought, the most sincerely at my professorly one-liners, hammering one another with burly elbows, straining their writing chairs to near breaking.

The women were different. Say what you will about equality of the sexes, but nothing was the same between males and females in my class. The women's reactions to my lecturing were much more guarded, and I could not decide if they were cooly appraising or calculating and posed. I shouldn't have been so cynical, but I was somewhat down on the gender. It would never have affected my grading, of course, but since the suffering my wife had caused, I looked at women more cautiously, with some mistrust and apprehension. I had no idea when or if I would start dating, but I did not think it would be very soon, even though I knew only a woman could heal me.

There were some very attractive young women in my freshman English class, and one in particular caught my attention. Her name was Bonnie Weber. She was from Maryland and I could not categorize her as Southern, for that state is borderline North and South, and her husky voice had no accent at all. When she laughed (feminists hate me), she laughed as heartily as one of the boys. From my lectern, I could see that she had a great figure, but her eyes made that asset insignificant. She had big green, grabbing eyes with long lashes. And when she looked at you, those eyes would not let yours wander to the halo of her soft blonde hair, or to her full breasts, trim waist, and strong, shapely legs. To make things tougher for me, she sat front row, center and seemed to watch every move I made, and to test every word. There was always one student like that in a class, one who kept you sharp. I would not make the mistake of some professors, of directing my lectures to her. But she did represent a challenge, and somehow kindled that spark I had felt when examining my naked form in the mirror on Mrs. Carswell's armoire. I needed that mirror, that image of elasticity, not brittleness.

Of course, I hadn't needed Cowpens Martin there to remind me I'd hit the dregs. I hadn't spoken to him that night, except to get the time. I made it to the drive-in before closing and got my chili cheeseburger, and I didn't see him again. I hoped he'd only been visiting, or even robbing the place. Anything but lodging.

After I finished calling the roll, the boy who had spat on Cowpens raised his hand and said, "S'cuse me, professor, but where are y'all from?" When I told him, he smiled wryly, looking as though he might step back and spit on me. But looks don't kill.

▽

Chapter 3

ON SATURDAY NIGHT, AFTER the first week of classes, Yates Sutherland held a faculty dinner party at his home. Yates had graduated from Sutherland College with me, in spite of his sleeping through most of his classes. I had to work for my degree and he had been the partyingest Southern gentleman of the decade. He never cracked a book, but his professors were afraid to flunk him. Yates's great grandfather had founded the town of Sutherland in 1854, the same year he built his first cotton mill on his farm. Then he founded the college so his son would have a place to go to school, "So's he kin larn whilst keepin' a hand in the bidness," was how Yates told it. Now Yates was president of the college, head of the board of trustees and, through the cotton mills he'd inherited, one of the wealthiest men in South Carolina. In short, he owned the college and the town.

Yates Sutherland's home was on a higher than usual rise in the rolling Piedmont at the outskirts of town. An elaborate gold-lettered sign on great brick pillars at the entrance to his long, winding driveway proclaimed the place *La Belle Colline*. I'd been in French classes with Yates, too, and I remembered how awful he was, not only in vocabulary and grammar, but in pathetic attempts at pronunciation with his heavy Southern drawl. Because of that, I figured that his wife must have named the property. From the tree-lined route to the house, I expected to emerge before a pillared mansion of antebellum splendor, a vision straight out of *Gone With The Wind*. Instead, I came upon huge gaslights, flaming like the torches in front of a Polynesian restaurant, which flickered wildly before a very new French provincial palace that was impressive in size but meretricious in gaudy appointments and bright red brick. It looked like a firehouse, on fire.

I pulled to the front door in my crappy Tempest, and a tall black man in a red velvet waistcoat offered to park my car. As I got out I said, "Brakes aren't so good, watch it," but he only nodded without the slightest trace of a smile or any such commiseration as, "I hears ya, bro, my own jalopy ain't bin runnin' so good." The smug dude probably had a brand-new Cadillac in the back.

My Tempest chugged away and I climbed an imposing pile of steps to the front door, where I was greeted by an even taller black man, also in a red velvet waistcoat. He smiled, and, for a moment, a wall of the whitest teeth I had ever seen distracted me from entering the Sutherland's grand foyer. When I did enter, I found myself under a glittering crystal chandelier of phenomenal proportions and quality that would have put Bessie Boatwright's punch bowl to shame— it probably had enough candlepower to illuminate the new Sutherland shopping mall they were building back in town.

"How do you do. I'm Mrs. Sutherland." A vision of Southern charm in a grandiose evening gown wafted toward me, gloved hand extended. I felt I should loop my tweedy, crumbum professor's necktie over the crystal chandelier and hang myself.

"How do you do," I muttered. "I'm Jim Harrington,

English professor and former classmate of your husband's."
It suddenly dawned on me who she was. She'd been a
student at Sutherland College when I was there, and she'd
had quite a reputation. Besides being homecoming queen,
she was supposed to have slept with the whole football team
and "porked" every SAE on campus. Perhaps I shouldn't
have related that, since college rumors can get quite out of
hand, and her extracurricular activities were certainly her
own business, but it struck me funny how one remembers
most of those juicy little tidbits after so many years. My
memory was helped, I suppose, because her appearance had
changed so little since those days. She still wore her hair in
a high bouffant, as so many Southern girls did then, so she
looked like a remnant of the early sixties, as if she had just
stepped out of the college yearbook. What was most amusing, though, was that it was obvious that she did not
remember me, that she was memorable and I was not. A
reputation of any sort was evidently inspiring compared with
the complete anonymity I'd achieved in my own mediocre
college career. Maybe if I had porked the entire woman's field
hockey team. . . . Well, dream on. . . .

"Yates is so excited, Mr. Harrington. He's told me all
about you."

"I hope not *all* about me, Mrs. Sutherland." I didn't know
why she was being so formal, but I decided to play along.

"It's all good, I can assure you, Mr. Harrington."

I was searching for something else to say when she
suddenly excused herself and drifted off to greet a couple who
had just entered. Glad to be let go, I walked into the
adjoining room, which was filled with the faculty having
cocktails. It was a large library with floor-to-ceiling shelves
that were carefully loaded with crisp, new, leatherbound
volumes of every great title in English literature. The sets of

books were so spiffy and so perfectly matched that I pulled
one off the shelf to see if it was real and not part of a facade.
It was real, but the binding was so stiff I was sure it had
never been opened. It was Anthony Trollope's *The Warden*
and, to be fair, I must say that I had never read it, but Yates
Sutherland certainly hadn't read it either. As I placed it
carefully back into its slot, I was approached by one of the
uniformed maids who bustled about serving hot hors
d'oeuvres and drinks. She offered me some kind of cheese
concoction, which I picked off of her silver tray with a
toothpick. It was delicious but it made me thirsty, and as I
looked around for a drink I ran smack into Yates Sutherland.
I had not seen him since our undergraduate days. The
arrangements for me to start teaching had been mostly over
the telephone, and I had only a quick, perfunctory interview
with the head of the English department before I started.
Yates had pulled all the strings, while out of town, and he
apparently ran the college with such autonomy that nobody
disputed his word.

"Well, ah'll be. Jim Harrington. You haven't changed a
bit, boy." His voice was as thick and sweet as Southern
Comfort, and he grasped my arm just above the elbow, where
it hurts. I was glad that he had seen me first, for I wouldn't
have recognized him if I had fallen over him. He'd become
very fat, and bald. Though he was my age, he looked at least
fifty, and ridiculous in an ill-fitting puce smoking jacket
with a white silk collar and a string tie. He slurped a
mouthful of the pungent-smelling, dark contents of his
glass, slapped me on the back so it hurt, and we shook hands.

"You look . . . great."

"Thanks for sayin' that, boy, but I have put on a little
weight." He patted his fat belly and slurped some more of
his drink.

"I want to thank you for. . . ."

"Forget it, boy. We like to hire those who've always been a part of our family."

"Well, I do appreciate—"

"I said, forget it." He held up his pudgy hand and then turned and started to walk away, beckoning for me to follow. As he walked ahead of me, I noticed he carried a heavy cane with a large gold ball for a handle. He seldom leaned on it, using it instead as a probe to clear a path through the crowd. We made the rounds as though in a little parade, Yates the drum major, a pudgy Mr. Pickwick, I the ragamuffin band.

Of course, I had already met those in the English department. Its head was a former professor of mine, Kenneth Coates. He was known to the students as "Kind Kenneth Coates," for his easy grading. His prattling on about Western North Carolinian lore (whatever that was—I never paid much attention), and his allegiance to scuppernong wine as a respectable libation were legend. He failed to sell the students on the latter because they all knew the gospel according to the Playboy Advisor: that all good wine has an unpronounceable French name and costs at least twelve dollars a bottle.

Besides Kenneth Coates, I knew only one other professor there. John Hill had been my geology professor when I was a senior. He was known to his students as "The Rock," and he had altered my entire view of the educational system in this country that depended so much on rote learning. We were mostly taught to memorize and parrot back information, but The Rock believed that insight, real knowledge, did not come from textbooks. "You can't understand deltaic sediment unless you stand in a delta," said The Rock, and he took his class to the French Broad River in the Blue Ridge Mountains, in January, and walked us barefoot into the freezing muck of the millennia. At the end of the class, we knew exactly what comprised a delta, and nobody ever forgot it. The Rock would have preferred us to read Sherlock Holmes instead of our geology textbook. "Find the clues, lads and ladies," he told us, "and put them together for yourselves." Yates reintroduced me to The Rock and, as we shook hands, I could tell I was as memorable to him as I'd been to Mrs. Sutherland. I forgave him, though, for in the years I'd been gone an uncountable parade of other mediocre students must have passed through his classes and marched with him into the freezing French Broad River. We finally finished our rounds and then Yates took me aside.

"Buncha old farts," he said. "Good to have some young blood here. Watcha been doin' with yourself, boy?"

I shrugged. "Teaching English."

"Don't be so modest. That's a noble callin'. I excelled in English, if you recall."

I did recall. Yates had slept through those classes too, and I couldn't resist the dig. "You did get through, thanks to Kind Kenneth Coates."

At first he scowled, and then broke into a sly grin. "Kind Kenny did help me a time or two."

"You and me, both."

"To tell you the truth"—he lowered his voice and put his face uncomfortably close to mine—"if I had my way, 'ceptin' for you of course, I'd lock up all these pro-fessors in a big study hall and make 'em listen to their own lectures a million times."

"The Rock's would be interesting," I said.

"You're right there, boy." He laughed and slapped my shoulder. We had all stayed awake for The Rock.

"You had some family trouble, didn't you, boy?"

"My wife and I split up."

"Hmmm." He stared at me while he swallowed the last of his drink and then plunked the empty glass down on the next silver tray that came by, not noticing, or caring probably, that it was a tray of cheese concoctions and not for drinks.

"Bring me another," he commanded, without ever looking at the maid.

"Nothing for me." I smiled at her, embarrassed at my host's rudeness.

"I never met your wife, did it?"

"She'd never been to the college. She was from New York."

"Pity."

"Nothing lasts forever."

"No. I mean you might shoulda gotten a Southern gal. They'll stick to you like glue."

"I might shoulda." I could see why he'd had trouble in English.

"You still playin' tinnis?" he asked me, still staring with his bulging, fat-man's eyes.

"As little as possible." I had played varsity tennis at Sutherland. Perhaps that was why he remembered me at all. We had never really been friends, only acquaintances at that small school, but I had played tennis and he had not participated in any sports, unless you count drinking and carousing.

"Why don't you coach the team? You were our number-one player, once."

"I don't think. . . ."

"It's extra money, boy. 'Sides, old Jim Seegars is tired of the job."

"Is he still teaching psychology?" Jim Seegars had coached the tennis team when I was there, when tennis was a bastard sport compared with football, basketball, and baseball, a status that probably hadn't changed. Seegars knew little about tennis, preferring golf, and he taught us psychological ploys such as his theory that doubles partners should always make end changes in tandem to give the illusion of unity and strength. His game plans of guile and one-upmanship were absurd and our poor team took a beating from almost every college we played, but Seegars insisted on the use of such gimmicks, as though volleys of Freudian voodoo could triumph over superior forehands and backhands.

"Jim Seegars is still hangin' in there," Yates said, and I looked around the room for my former coach.

"He ain't here yet, boy, but how about you coachin'?"

"I'll think on it." I unconsciously used that Southern idiom, and then realized it when Yates chuckled. I wondered if he was amused because I had sounded so much like Scarlet O'Hara, or if the noncommittal phrase was, to him, a positive indication that I would coach the team.

"You think on it, boy." He slapped my shoulder again and then spied a new face in the room and mercifully left me without another word. I remembered that I didn't like him.

It was difficult to get near the bar, a glass and brass menagerie that made me wish I was back at Elmer's Trade-winds. The place was becoming packed with the pickled brain trust of Sutherland College, some fifty faculty members and their spouses, all moving and talking like molasses, bantering bits of arcanum, and clustering like the nuts in warm pecan pie. I was in a foreign land. With a bourbon and ginger finally in my mitts, I moved about the high-ceilinged room, examining more of the books. I stopped before a giant gilt-framed portrait that hung over the fireplace. Sipping my drink I surveyed the glowering countenance of Yates Sutherland's great grandfather, noting a strong resemblance to that old religion professor I had once endured. Then I sensed someone studying the dark canvas with me and I turned, to be grabbed by the green eyes of Bonnie Weber, the girl from the front row of my freshman English class.

"Some serious dude." She nodded at the painting but did not let my eyes leave hers.

"That he is, Miss Weber."

"Bonnie."

"What are you doing at this dull faculty party, Bonnie? Lost your faculties?" I raised an eyebrow to add punch to the poor pun, and Bonnie laughed in a voice so husky I expected her to elbow me like one of the football players at the rear of my classroom and chortle, "That's a good un, perfesser."

"By the way, I'm Jim, except in class," I allowed.

"I'm the entertainment, Jim, except in class." She smiled and showed her even, pretty teeth.

At first I imagined that she was blatantly coming on to me, then she explained what she meant by entertainment.

"I'm going to sing," she said, "and Mrs. Sutherland will accompany me on the piano. She teaches music at the college, you know."

"What will you sing?"

"Oh, a little Cosi Fan Tutti and . . ."

"My favorite."

"Really?"

"I like everything by Freddy Fender."

Bonnie liked my joke and gave me more of her hearty Wife-of-Bath laughter. Mrs. Sutherland might have thought me crude, if she knew Freddy Fender was a fat, greasy fugitive from a mariachi band, or if she admitted to knowing. But Bonnie proved to be a Yankee-Marylander, able to appreciate irreverence toward the classics and culture, those commodities being too unstable in the South to denigrate.

"Want to look around?" she asked.

"I've been looking around." I made a sour face at the family portrait.

"I mean the whole place. Mrs. Sutherland said I should take a tour of the house, and I'm sure it's okay for you to come too."

"Let's go," I said enthusiastically, relieved to escape the den of learned men and women. We wandered off together, passing first through the grand foyer, where I was very much impressed by the size and elaborateness of the spiral staircase. I had paid little attention to it when I first came in that evening; the crystal chandelier and Mrs. Sutherland had distracted me. The staircase was one of those double-spiral ones, with ornate banisters that curled seductively up from opposite sides of the foyer to a large landing at the top that looked out onto the bulk of that chandelier. Bonnie wanted to go upstairs first, and I agreed.

"You can probably get a good suntan up there from this thing." I nodded at the chandelier. She laughed, and my comment set the tone for the tour.

We nosed about the Sutherland mansion, sharing asides with regard to the hodgepodge of fantasy rooms we found, each the product of too much money and a flighty sense of decor. We named the rooms: The Peach Pit, The Cotton Candy Room, Boll Weevil Den, Sidney Lanier Lounge. We called the master bedroom "The Louisiana Purchase" because it looked as though it had been transported intact from a New Orleans whorehouse. I decided that Mrs. Sutherland, the decorator, or perpetrator, had made each room a caricature of the genteel, gracious features that were my fond image of Dixie. If I hadn't known that Yates had come from relatively old money, I would have surmised that he was nouveau riche, or that he was a New Jersey gangster and that La Belle Colline was a plasticized catering concern in Hoboken.

When we returned to the party, three black maids were moving about, announcing that dinner was to be served. We funneled into an immense dining room and Bonnie and I sat next to each other at the longest banquet table I had ever seen. The dining room itself was a razzmatazz version of the Hall of Mirrors at Versailles. There were no less than seven, count 'em, seven glittering crystal chandeliers in a row over the dining table. As we were being seated, I thought if someone didn't turn the lights down I would have to go to my car for my Ray-Bans. The room's narrowness, compared with its length, made me feel as if we were in a Pullman car, and spiffy porters ladled something suspiciously thick and green from fine china bowls.

I enjoyed Bonnie more than the dinner, and the wine the best of all. I was getting sloshed, but I wasn't alone. At the head of the table, Yates spoke loudly and gestured wildly to a group of cronies, or toadies, I didn't know which. They were probably just a bunch of nodding heads too fuzzy with bourbon and wine to care about being talked at. Bonnie took it easy with the drinks because she had to sing for her supper. I wondered if she could warble through Cosi Fan Tutti with a buzz on but, to that drunken crowd, it wouldn't have mattered if she did selections from Waylon and Willie, or improvised a "Contata for Tank Displacement" from the ROTC training manual.

Between courses, Yates stood and tapped his wine glass. "I want to welcome y'all back," he said, "and to welcome those who are just now joining, or rejoining"—he glanced at me—"our big, happy family."

Somebody shouted, "Hear, hear," and all raised their glasses and drank.

"You're not stoppin' me that easy." Yates raised one pudgy finger and there was nervous laughter here and there.

"Brevity is the soul of wit," someone called out.

"Brevity is the antithesis of tenure." Yates shot the caller a dirty look and the room fell silent. It was apparent that some of the professors were afraid of him, and that he was essentially a rude man. "As I was sayin'," he continued, "I want to welcome y'all back, and remind you that Sutherland College has grown substantially, not only in student enrollment and the capability of our physical plant to handle that growth, which includes two new residence halls and a brand-new gymnasium, but in stature among other small colleges in the South, and in the country." Someone yawned, and the servers shifted anxiously, wanting to get on with the next course. "Now, we're ranked in the top five academically, and last year our football team was, as you surely know, runner-up in the NAIA national championship.

"Hear, hear," someone shouted again. Everyone drank and, thinking Yates was finished, resumed their conversations. Yates just stood there. His eyes narrowed and his face grew red and, after fumbling with a soup spoon, he hit his wine glass so hard that it shattered. The room fell dead silent and Yates, breathing hard, looked as though he might go into a tirade. But he managed to compose himself and, after a pause during which the success of the evening hung in jeopardy, he stated flatly, "I only wanted to add that Sutherland College is on the move." At that moment, two maids rushed over and cleaned up the broken glass and replaced it with another. Yates watched regally, weaving slightly, and then a server poured him some more wine. Yates pulled the glass away before it was filled, so the server was left pouring wine onto the table. He began to wipe it up but Yates waved him away and raised his glass. "To our big, happy family." He grinned. The assemblage drank again and then waited a few moments to see if he had anything to add, but he simply sat and resumed his conversation with those next to him. Soon everyone else did the same.

As the dinner progressed, I became aware of my status, and Bonnie's, from our place at the table. We were right at the center, farthest from the principals, Yates and his wife, at the opposite ends. From our median juncture, the faculty was divided antipodally, with Yates drawing the business and science factions and his wife pulling the humanities. Bonnie and I could have gone either way to spread conversation but, beyond the magnetic fields at either end of that very long table, we drew like vagrant monopoles to each other. Merrily we discoursed on everything from Ozawa to the Ozarks, through umpteen courses of oeufs en gelée to gazpacho. I was feeling no pain. The rest of the dinner went smoothly and Yates had no more outbursts.

After a flaming dessert that nobody needed, and assorted liqueurs that nobody should have been allowed, the assemblage retired to the music room to hear Bonnie sing and Mrs. Sutherland play. Left alone, I waltzed to a seat in what Bonnie and I had previously named "Alice Tully in Wonderland Hall," for its Liberace-inspired white Steinway and candelabra, lavish silk curtains and various busts of old composers that were placed everywhere, in specially lighted little alcoves and on pedestals and shelves about the room. As Mrs. Sutherland grandly seated herself at the piano, I focused on the diamond necklace she wore. I was just catching up with Sutherland overkill, appreciating their possessions that individually slapped you in the face, but that collectively were blinding. The stones in her necklace looked so heavy that I feared should she lean into the arpeggio she would crash into the keyboard. She didn't though. And she was an adequate accompanist, for all I knew, but Bonnie's contralto renditions seemed superb. She was roundly applauded and, through the course of the program, I counted only three who had fallen asleep. They finished to a standing ovation, which was prompted by Yates, and the bar reopened and the party resumed.

It was late when Bonnie asked me for a ride back to her dorm. She'd come by a car that Mrs. Sutherland had sent but she didn't want to bother the hostess for another ride when the party was still going full force. I said I'd take her, and we quickly thanked the Sutherlands and slipped out the front door. The doorman brought my car within a minute, and it announced its arrival with tortured metallic groans from the engine compartment that were reminiscent of the eerie song of the humpback whale. The water pump, I diagnosed, and if it gave out before I got my first paycheck, I had a problem.

Bonnie and I climbed in and, as we drove, the car's moaning turned to canary-like tweets and then stopped. I would have forgotten the sounds anyway. I'm sure that my drunken state enhanced it, but Bonnie's nearness distracted me and I had never been so aware of the sensual power of a mere speaking voice. When she talked, her throaty contralto was full of salubrious messages from her pumping diaphragm, messages that had been nurtured deep in her petal-pink lungs and then sucked slowly up and thrust across her throbbing vocal chords—the sounding box of sex. Her splendid organs brought new meaning to the term "visceral excitement." My own organs paled so in comparison. My nasal New York-ese had always precluded any vocal massaging of wenches into the reckless abandonment of their mores. I listened to her and, when my Tempest pulled up in front of her dorm and I killed the engine, I regretted that she would have to go.

We sat silent a moment. I savored a light dizziness and, when Bonnie finally spoke, it seemed she hovered immediately above me.

"Thank you for the ride," she said.

"My pleasure." I smiled and expected her to jump out of the car and dash into her dorm. But to my surprise she leaned over and gave me a quick kiss on the lips. In my fuzzy state, the kiss seemed unreal and I didn't know what to say.

"I sing other than opera," she declared. Then, in low volume but forceful all the same, she began to sing the raunchy "stripper's song."

"Let me entertain you. . . ." she growled, reaching out a hand and loosening my necktie.

I wanted her . . . but I didn't. I wasn't ready . . . and I couldn't. I was her teacher . . . and it was too soon. She finished her chorus and glared at me with those big green eyes. Then, parting her full lips, those soft portals of Cosi Fan Tutti, she slowly ran her tongue across her perfect teeth. I thought again about the wonderful emanation of her sound, her pink lungs and throbbing vocal chords. Then I shook my head and the wine-induced fuzziness cleared long enough for me to tell her. "This won't help your grade, Miss Weber."

Undaunted, she cooed, "I'll grade you, professor," and fussed with my tie some more.

"Good night," I said sternly, in the most professorly manner I could muster. Then I reached past her and shoved open the passenger-side door.

"Thanks again for the ride." She smiled as though nothing had happened and pranced out of the car and into her dorm.

$\triangledown$

Chapter 4

SUNDAY MORNING CAME DOWN hard. My head split and my mouth was as dry as New Jersey in August. I cracked first one eye open and then the other. Shafts of the normally innocent, playful kind of light that hails the beginning of a golden, glorious day blitzed around the window curtain and sizzled into my brain. I cursed the last glass of wine I'd drunk at Yates Sutherland's party. Then I got up. It was easy. Just a quick roll that cleaved me from between the sheets like a rock popping out from a shift in the San Andreas fault. But the aftershock, that was the stunner. I stood trembling naked on the floor. My skin was cold and clammy, and thunder and lightning inside my skull tested the brittle bone casing and threatened to split it open. Then I made the mistake of breathing, and all the benign little particles that were suffused in the morning light gathered into a single white-hot vortex that roared up my nasal passages to fuel the fire inside my cranium. Tenderly, as one eases into a very hot bath, I drew on some clothes and shuffled ever so slowly out of my room toward the rooming house kitchen, for a try at making some instant coffee.

The hall and the kitchen were empty. I was glad. I needed all my energy to fill the community kettle and to light the

old stove's gas burner. I struck a match and regretted the
oxygen it would use, valuable fuel that could help my horrid
condition. Never again, I swore over and over until the kettle
finally rattled to a boil. Ah, coffee, I thought as the frenzied,
heat-speeded molecules of hydrogen and oxygen ejaculated
onto the brown dust I'd shoveled into one of Mrs. Carswell's
chipped ceramic mugs. Coffee would cure me, I prayed—
along with the peace and quiet of a slow, Carolina Sunday
morning. I remembered those mornings: how peaceful they
were when the college slept off its hangovers. When the
campus was strewn with empty Rebel Yell bottles and I,
much better off as an undergraduate, and much more sober,
would blithely slip down to the college cafeteria and join a
handful of other sensible souls for early breakfast.

I stirred in some milk I found in the refrigerator and was
about to sit down at Mrs. Carswell's old kitchen table to
savor the quiet and the coffee's healing aroma when, suddenly, Cowpens Martin's turnip-green twang cut me from
behind.

"How're y'all this fine morning!"

I cringed and shook, and scalding fluid slopped out of my
mug onto my thumb.

"Eny bawlin' water left in that there kettle?" He grinned.

I squinted at the pain that somehow went directly from
my thumb to my head. Then I sat down at the small kitchen
table and ignored him.

"Don't mind me." He checked the kettle. "I kin see you
ain't awake yet."

He fumbled around and made some coffee for himself, and
then sat down next to me.

"Mind if I set a spell?"

I said nothing, hoping he'd go away, but he stayed while
I took a sip of coffee.

"'Preciate it." He offered his scrawny hand and I wished I could pour a little boiling water on it to get him back, but I shook with him just the same and the gesture pumped more pressure into my aching head.

I mumbled my name. I hadn't introduced myself the other night, when I first saw him in the kitchen and was in such a hurry to get a chili cheeseburger. I'd hoped then, as now, that he was an illusion. I'd already sunk low enough, and his mere existence was too grim a reminder of how low I could really go, and how I might have to finish out my life if I couldn't recover. Maybe I should have stayed in Saratoga Springs.

I forced myself to look at him and noticed that he at least looked better than he had under the pinball machine at Elmer's Tradewinds Lounge. But not much better.

"Pleased to have yew aboard," he mindlessly rambled on, stirring milk and huge dollops of sugar into the mud he'd made. "I'm from jest up the road. Towna the same name. Cowpens, that is, not Martin."

I nodded, as though interested, but dipping my head almost destroyed me, so I half smiled instead.

"Bin livin' here, though, at Mrs. Carswell's fer a good spell. Jest down the hall there." He pointed a bony, crooked finger toward the other end of the hall from my room, and my worst fears were confirmed. I tried to look uninterested, to squelch him, and solemnly sipped my coffee.

"Yew ain't with the college, are yew?" He was undeterred, obviously compelled to carry the conversational ball.

"How did you know?" I asked snidely.

"Shoot." He grinned, oblivious to my rudeness, and disclosed a surprisingly good set of teeth. "Now don't think—I ain't no de-e-tective. I dun ast Mrs. Carswell." He grinned some more and, when I failed to answer, he added, "She's a good woman." He seemed to reflect a moment on Mrs.

Carswell's virtue, or whatever, and finally took a sip of his coffee.

"Dang, that's hot!" he yelped. "How kin yew drink her so dang hot."

"Skill." With a little pain I raised one eyebrow.

"That's droll, Jim." He slapped one knee and emphasized the word *droll* as if it were some kind of a shibboleth necessary to talk to college people.

"Actually, I can only drink coffee when it's piping hot." My words were measured and stern, as though I lectured a stubborn student.

"I said that was droll, Jim." He still tried to get credit for his special word.

"Yes. Droll. That's a good word. You have been to college too." I couldn't help myself.

"Hell, no, I ain't never bin to no college." He bristled. "But I know a thing er two."

I smirked, and regretted it, recalling what one of my professors had said in my freshman year at Sutherland College. The man had more degrees than all of the faculty put together but he offered that, "An educated man is one who knows something, and who can talk about it." Perhaps he was overly simplistic, and naive, but it made me wonder. Certainly he'd devoured all the great books and examined the noblest thoughts. And did it come down to this: to the prattling of a lost little man like Cowpens Martin? Were the answers to the great questions of the universe to be found in anyone with some life experience and a mouth? Then I remembered something else that professor had said, that once one had been to Paris, every other city was just like Sutherland. And I recalled, too, the quizzical looks of Southerners in that class who thought Paris, Georgia, wasn't all that great.

"Where're y'all from?" He blew on his coffee, and his inquisitive manner compelled me, inveterate teacher that I was, to answer in spite of my discomfort.

"Saratoga Springs, New York, most recently, but I was born and reared in New York City."

At first, he was incredulous that anyone could leave the great state of New York for such an outpost as Sutherland, South Carolina. Or maybe he was just being polite. Anyway, he wanted to know about New York City, and I answered his questions as briefly and as politely as I could. Though my hangover was still very much with me, I began to think I might survive. I stopped his questioning by making myself a second cup of coffee, and by asking him about the town of Cowpens.

"Ain't much," he admitted, "but it has some interestin' history. Cowpens was the site of a great victory for us in the Revolutionary War. Why, our boys dun whipped up on a high-toned British general named Banaster Tarleton, and I had family in that there fight."

He knew something, and could talk about it, and I listened to how our ragamuffin troops of farmers and country boys took the starch out of the Brits in a cornfield on a cold January dawn.

"Smit 'em with our squirrel guns, we did." He talked as though he'd been there, as though his life and that makeshift battlefield of so long ago were not so terribly far apart.

He'd have rambled on, but the pressure in my head seemed to build in proportion to the length of the story, so I stopped him again by asking, "Who else lives here? You're the only one I've met."

"A prefesser like yerself, Jim, was here for a short while . . . but he left. Then, there's Warren . . . but he's away." He seemed pleased to go in any direction I wanted, to expound upon any topic I chose. It was as though I were a baseball coach, hitting fungoes, and he were a rookie, eager to field them all.

"Warren owns that little pink T'bird yew mighta seen out back."

I had seen the car, a 1957 Thunderbird, one of the rare little two-seaters, with a shocking pink body, white convertible top, full fender skirts, chrome headlight bezels and, to gild the lily, a cumbersome continental kit protruding from the rear bumper.

"Car's a classic," I said, "and it looks to be in perfect shape."

He nodded in agreement, as though I spoke of the virtue of Mrs. Carswell.

"I'm not crazy about the color," I added, "but it would bring a pretty price."

"Why, ole Warren ain't never gonna sell that pimpmobile!" He laughed, slapped his skinny thigh, and nearly tipped his coffee mug over.

"I guess this Warren's a real ladies' man." I smiled, pleased to think that someone with a sharp car, manners, and a way with women might live there, not just this woeful little redneck. This time, however, Cowpens stopped me short.

"Hell, no. Ole Warren dun bought that car fer one of his boyfriends."

"Boyfriends? He's not . . . "

"Queer as a three-dollar bill. Don't worry though, Jim, he won't bother yew. He ain't never bothered me, neither. He knows I'd hand him his dang head."

The Piedmont had just gotten seedier and I, at a loss for words, went back to the subject of the car.

"You said he bought it for his boyfriend?"

"And the sucker up and left him." He nodded with a knowing smirk. "Now Warren says he's gonna keep it and run the ungrateful bastard over with it, if he ever comes back. Ain't that somethin', Jim?"

"That's droll." The story was getting long, but I noticed that my headache had softened to a dull throb.

"He means it." Cowpens shook his head and looked concerned. "And he's too good a man to have a murder charge on him." His coffee had cooled down and he drank it in one swallow.

"Then you two are . . . friends?"

"Yup. And he's the same age as me, fifty-two. But yew think he'd settle down and stop chasin' after them young boys."

"Where is he now?"

"The boyfriend? Who in the hell knows?"

"I mean Warren."

"Oh. He got drunk a few days ago out at the Greenville/Spartanburg jetport and, jest as purty as yew please, hopped a plane fer New York. Didn't even have no luggage. Said he'd met a coupla sailors. 'Seafood,' he called 'em. Ain't that droll, Jim?"

It was oddly amusing and I chuckled, but it hurt my head.

"Enyways, he called me from a phone booth, pumpin' in quarters, tellin' me not to worry. Sailors, I kin imagine. Now what the hell was sailors doin' in a jetport, in the middle of the dang state?"

He made some more coffee and, genuinely concerned, went on about his friend. I wondered if the professor who had lived there before me had left because Warren had made advances, or because he was repulsed by Cowpens, or both.

As the morning wore on, and my hangover wore off a little more, Cowpens Martin came into focus. If he was fifty-two, as he'd said, it was either his baseball age or he had far more mileage on him than Warren's thirty-year-old T'bird. His narrow, ferret face was weathered to a thousand wrinkles. When he asked if I minded him smoking, and then produced a tobacco pouch from the frayed pocket of his Western-style shirt and rolled a cigarette, I watched a moribund Marlboro man, the shadow of a cowpuncher, cadaverous despite the twinkle in his eye and his spindle-fingered alacrity at making his own coffin nails. He ran his gray tongue along the paper's glued edge, sealed it with a flourish without losing a trace of tobacco, and offered the result to me. I thanked him but declined. He fumbled with the matches though, and as I watched him light up, my attention was drawn to his tobacco pouch, which was dried and crinkled old leather of some sort. It made me think of a movie I'd once seen where Karl Malden had a tobacco pouch he'd made from cutting off an Indian woman's breast. Cowpens inhaled deeply, tossed the match into Mrs. Carswell's kitchen sink, and quickly stuffed the tobacco pouch back into his shirt pocket.

"What do yew teach at the college, Jim?"

"English."

"Don't most of the students speak it already?" He grinned slyly, and I wanted to tell him that was droll, but I didn't find it all that amusing.

"I teach English literature. Thoreau, Wordsworth . . . "

"I don't mean to butt in, but do yew also teach them children what they own words is worth, and how to sell 'em?"

He had me there, and it was a clever pun from a man of little formal education, from a hopeless drunk who probably spent most of his evenings passed out under a pinball machine.

"I do teach creative writing, if that's what you mean."

He furrowed his brows, looking thoughtful a moment, and

suddenly I was on the defensive. Now he was the coach with the fungo bat, and I had to field them all. He inhaled more of his cigarette, and carefully exhaled away from me, and rather than suffer any further critique of my college curriculum, I hastily took the opportunity to ask him what he did for a living.

"I'm a flag waver," he replied.

"I'm patriotic too, but does it pay well?"

"Nooo, I wave the flag fer the road gangs, so's the traffic kin pass."

"Oh, you work for the highway department."

"It ain't as glamorous as it sounds, Jim. I got say-so on that job, but I spend mosta the day kickin' rocks and eatin' dust."

"That's like my job," I told him, trying more to be clever than condescending.

"Come on, now."

"No, I spend most of my day inculcating, er, kicking knowledge into my students and then eating crow when I find out most of them are smarter than I am, or was at that age."

He inhaled a long time and then shrugged, and I knew I wasn't always amusing either.

"Job's a job," he said, smoke rolling out of his nostrils.

"I'll drink to that." I swallowed the remainder of my coffee, and realized that our conversation was over.

I went back to my room, thinking it might not be so bad there after all, and lay down on my bed. The sunlight through my window had become pleasant again, and a soft breeze drifted in and pushed my hangover further back into memory. In fact, it was nearly gone, if I didn't move, or think of Cowpens Martin.

⬝

Chapter 5

By THAT SUNDAY AFTERNOON I had recovered enough from my hangover to meet an old friend at Sutherland Park to play tennis. I had not seen or spoken to Carlos Garcia since my undergraduate days, more than sixteen years ago, when we had double-dated, or cruised around the town looking for girls each Saturday night, and then met to play tennis the next afternoon. Though public, Sutherland park had seemed our private little club at the outskirts of town, beyond reach of the college, in a relatively new but attractive neighborhood of ranch-style homes. The tennis courts themselves were nestled in a secluded area, surrounded by trees down near a lake, away from a small parking lot. There were only four courts, but at least one was always available in those days, when tennis was still somewhat of an esoteric sport, at least in that part of the South.

Sometimes a small crowd from the neighborhood would watch us play, as Carlos had been a ranking player in Brazil, his native country, and I was good enough to play first singles for Sutherland College's mediocre tennis team.

I was right on time for our meeting, but Carlos was already there grinning from the driver's seat of a brand new Merce-des-Benz convertible as my car, again whining like a hump-

49

back whale, clamored into the little parking lot.

Carlos said he'd attended college in Brazil, before coming to this country, where he and his family first set up their small jewelry business in Queens, New York. Their business had existed only marginally there, so they took one more chance and moved everything to Sutherland on no more recommendation than blindly sticking a pin into a map. At least that's what Carlos and his father liked to say, and they chuckled at my amazement. They'd gutted and refurbished an old pool parlor on Sutherland's main street, and built elaborate showcases for their custom-made jewelry. Their timing was perfect, since shortly thereafter downtown Sutherland was completely renovated and Main Street was closed to traffic and turned into an attractive shopping mall. Business flourished for Carlos and his father, who worked as a team. Carlos handled the customers and designed the jewelry to order, and his father, an old craftsman, made the pieces and did repair. There were other jewelry stores and pawnshops in Sutherland, but they only sold standard, catalog items, while the Garcias alone did fine custom work that appealed in the area that was becoming known as "The New South." Industry was moving in from the north, to cheaper land and labor, and there was a surge in homebuilding, and a hunger among the expanded, wealthier populace for some of the luxuries that the big cities offered. Sutherland still had a long way to go, but it and the Garcias were on the move.

Carlos looked happy and healthy in his Mercedes, only a little more bald than when I'd last seen him. I knew he was at least forty, though he'd never admit it, and I recalled that he'd always looked forty, even sixteen years ago.

"You must be selling a lot of Mickey Mouse watches," I called out as I pulled up next to his shiny car.

"Our hottest item, man." His Brazilian accent was still quite evident.

We jumped from our cars and shook hands. He looked as trim as ever, and I admit I hoped the jewelry business had at least slowed him down, since I was way out of practice for tennis with anyone good. He patted the front fender of my Tempest, and then licked his finger and rubbed to see if it would shine, but the old finish showed up as faded as ever.

"You holding onto a classic here?"

"I keep it because of the squeaking sound. It drives women wild."

Without smiling, he told me it was the water pump and that I'd better fix it soon. He'd always been serious about automobiles and image, and had to own the "right" car, something new and fancy. He'd been poor in Brazil and had owned only wrecks like mine. To his embarrassment, his father would tell me how they saved the used motor oil in barrels, until the impurities settled out, and then put it back in the engine. It bothered him that I didn't care what I drove, and I'd had worse clunkers than that Tempest in my undergraduate days.

"Remember my old Plymouth?" I teased.

"Stick with me." He was still serious. "I'll show you what car to buy."

"Show me the money first. I'm just a college professor, you know."

"There's a Sutherland professor who drives a new BMW, man." He looked surprised that I didn't know it, and that I didn't aspire to the same.

"He must owe his soul," I told him, half-serious but looking concerned enough for the poor professor's finances so he felt I was a lost cause, for the moment. He finally smiled and we chatted about other, equally important items as we walked toward the tennis courts. It's a strange phenomenon that certain friends can be completely out of contact for long periods of time, and immediately reestablish their old relationships as soon as they meet again. So it seemed, at that moment, that Carlos and I had never missed a Sunday afternoon of tennis in the last sixteen years.

"How's your game, man?" He put his arm around my shoulder as we took an empty court.

"Take it easy on me. I haven't played."

"Hah! I've heard that before and you whipped my ass."

I shook my head, and then asked, "Have you brought balls? I don't have any."

"I've heard that before too." He laughed and popped the top off a new can he'd been holding under one arm. He was always generous with tennis balls. When it was my turn to bring them, they were usually used ones I'd scrounged from the college athletic department, or saved from one of my team matches. And though mine were still quite serviceable for a practice match, Carlos always opened a new can.

We took opposite sides of the friendly green asphalt court we'd trod so often before. We stretched a little in the sun's warmth, a day we'd take for Indian summer in New York but one they took for granted at that time of the year in South Carolina. Then we hit, and it felt good. Moving blood and light perspiration completely erased my hangover. Though I was way out of practice, my strokes were smooth and relaxed. I was able to keep up with Carlos and return his shots crisply and accurately. We fiddled with speed and the spin, and adjusted the depth. We established a rhythm that musicians and lovers find only after they've been harmonizing a very long time. I knew I wouldn't last as long as Carlos, though. Despite his thinning hair and circles under his eyes that more reflected a family trait than age and physical condition, his legs were still toned and heavily muscled. And though he was short and somewhat narrow-shouldered, he could hit remarkably hard.

Carlos played with a Latin passion that, coupled with his quick temper and his small, beady brown eyes and large nose, often made him appear a comic character. He'd strut and pace and jump and shake when he got mad on the tennis court, and off. Once, he tried to impress a group of young girls who watched us play. He won some furious points that would have beaten John McEnroe or the devil, and had the girls entranced. But he ruined it all when, in changing sides, he paid too much attention to the admiring gallery and the hem of his shorts caught on the net post and ripped completely and loudly up the side. The girls and I laughed hysterically, but Carlos was mortified and couldn't win another point.

Although no one was waiting for our court, we hit for only an hour. We didn't push it past our limits—Carlos was out of practice too—or break the spell by playing games or a set. When we were finished we sat on a bench that overlooked the small lake, and talked.

"You're hitting great, man," he said.

"I guess you never forget." I noticed that a small blister had developed between my thumb and forefinger.

"Like fucking, man. Who forgets that."

"I've forgotten." I shrugged, and picked at my blister.

At first he laughed, then he became very serious.

"You mean your wife," he said.

I had told him on the phone, when we made the tennis date. I had to give him a reason for coming back alone.

"I'm trying to forget her." I'd even told him she'd run off with another guy.

"I couldn't forget." His eyes narrowed. "I'd have killed her, or him, or both."

"You can get away with that in Brazil."

"Here too, man."

I wanted to change the sordid subject so I went, as usual, for a joke.

"I'm glad the one thing you never got is a Southern accent after all this time."

"And I'm glad you came to your senses, man, and got out of that shitty New York."

With those words, we shifted to an hour of idle chatter, to a review of the old days and enjoyment of the afternoon as we had so many times before on that bench overlooking the courts and the lake, in the shade of the Southern pine.

Carlos still lived with his family. It seemed remarkable to me that he hadn't married and established a home of his own, but I told him he was better off. I didn't tell him, though, that I now lived with the likes of Cowpens Martin.

"Come to dinner this evening," he urged. "Churrasco, matambra, and plenty of beer."

That salty, delicious Brazilian barbecue was a Sunday ritual for the Garcias, and I'd shared it with them many times. I accepted immediately. I told him I'd go back to my apartment and change first, and we stiffly got up from the bench and walked back up the slope to our cars.

"We're getting older, I think," I said.

"Speak for yourself, man."

"I'm not so old that I don't remember Jody."

"Sure." Carlos suddenly looked sour and tossed the used tennis balls into a refuse container we passed.

"Those are still good." I walked over and picked the balls out.

"Forget them, man," he said with a sneer. "They're used."

"I need 'em."

"Suit yourself." He shrugged and we continued toward the cars.

"But Jody," I asked, "Did you ever see her after I left?"

Jody was my girlfriend when I was a Sutherland senior. We'd been serious about each other, but I simply left her and the South for good when I graduated. It wasn't quite that simple, really. I'd thought of her often, through the good times and the bad times with my wife, wondering what I'd missed. I even called her a few times from up north, before I was married, and planned to visit. And once, or twice, I'd thought of asking her to come live with me.

Carlos climbed into his Mercedes and put on the gold Rolex he'd casually left on the shift console.

"She was broken up about you, man, when you left."

"You left that watch in this open car?"

"This is the South, not that shitty New York." He grinned and started his car and called out, "See you around five," as he drove away.

I made it to the Garcia's home by five, and was impressed by what I saw. When they'd first come to Sutherland, they lived in an inexpensive apartment complex called Crystal Springs. Now they had a jewel of a home, a large, modern ranch house in one of Sutherland's ritziest sections.

The kindly Mr. and Mrs. Garcia greeted me as though I were a returning son. Their faltering English effused love and concern and, where vocabulary failed, the warmest communication came from their eyes. They were so unlike Carlos, who had learned the language too well, who had the American argot down pat and, though he still had a strong Brazilian accent, had the nuance to make his mouth his principal communicator: his sly tongue could make liars of his eyes.

Carlos had a sister, who was omnipresent, and two younger brothers who were never around. The sister was fast pushing forty and fair certain to become an old maid. In spite of the fact that all of the Garcias were short and compact, she was cursed with an ungainly height. And to make matters worse, her figure was sloppy, with no bust, shapeless hips, and thick legs that I'd often heard Carlos refer to as "bologna legs." Unfortunately, the only Garcia family trait she shared was a large nose. I wondered how she related to Southern men, and if she'd have been married if she lived in Brazil, or back in Queens. I felt that men down South were fussier about their women, and insecure with anyone from out of their realm.

His sister may have been a convent candidate, but Carlos was a dating fool. He chased every woman in town and had few reservations with regard to looks, class, or age. He'd always been promiscuous, at least to my way of thinking, and I wondered if he'd settled down since he'd become a wealthy burgher and a big fish in the little catfish hole called Sutherland.

We sat at a picnic table in the backyard and watched Mr. Garcia prepare the meat for barbecue. He wound the churrasco—long, slender strips of lean meat sliced from the matambra, the rib section of beef—around wooden skewers and placed them on the fire. The smell of the cooking meat aroused our hunger, and we quaffed icy cans of beer and talked more of old times while we waited. Amid curling charcoal smoke and coming dusk, we ate heartily and mulled over the progress of the last sixteen years. The Garcias were flush with undisguised pride at their accomplishments and I characteristically understated my impecunious achievements.

"Is Yates Sutherland a customer of yours?" I asked.

"Sure, man," Carlos boasted. "I designed a brooch for his wife, just last week."

"Hoo-hoo," Mr. Garcia sang, "thir-ty-two diamonds. No mosquito shit, either."

Mrs. Garcia chortled, as though her upper plate might fall out, but she covered her mouth in time and blushed with embarrassment at her husband's language. "Mosquito shit" was how he referred to the size of tiny diamonds, and ones a little larger he called "fly shit."

"Big rocks, man," Carlos concurred. "Each one perfect."

Mr. Garcia knitted his brow and nodded.

"That brooch is worth half a mil, easy," Carlos added.

"Stop me if I'm being nosy," I said, "but does the customer pay up front for the diamonds, or does the jeweler have to sell his home and car to make such a brooch?"

Carlos cackled like a hyena and nearly fell off the picnic table bench. Then, while he parents looked askance, he recovered and said cryptically, "We have our ways. . . ."

"It's really a little of both, Jim," said Mr. Garcia.

"I guess I shouldn't have broached the subject," I said.

Carlos laughed and Mr. and Mrs. Garcia looked quizzically at me. Then, Carlos explained the pun in rapid Portuguese, and they all acknowledged it in translation-delayed, canned laughter. I made a mental note to save that kind of pun for my English classes, where they'd at least respond immediately with catcalls and hoots.

Suddenly, Mr. Garcia looked at his watch and got up from the table.

"Come, querida, it's time," he said to his wife. "Please excuse us," he said to me.

I stood and thanked them for their hospitality, while Carlos snickered and squirmed on his seat. His father shot him a wry look, and then suppressed a smile at the private joke they shared. He took his wife's hand and marched off into the house, leaving only Carlos and me.

"They're going to watch *Archie Bunker's Place*." Carlos laughed.

"What's wrong with that?"

"My dad's embarrassed. He doesn't like anybody to know. We knew a guy in Queens like Archie, a real American."

I did not understand his amusement, nor his father's embarrassment. I guessed that Archie Bunker was something to stay away from if you had come up from the blue-collar middle class.

"There are plenty of Archies down here," I shrugged, trying to make light of it, "with a little different accent."

"But they watch it religiously, man," he sneered, and I knew it was he who had made his father embarrassed.

"They're Lutherans," I kidded. "But I forgot. You're a lothario."

He stared at me, expressionless. His English wasn't good enough to get all of my puns, or perhaps not all of them deserved recognition. I was about to explain, when Mrs. Garcia poked her head out the back door and called, "Carlos, you have a visitor. She's coming around the side."

We turned at the same time and looked at the corner of the house to see who would come around it. A slender young woman emerged, but it was near dark and I could not make out her features. As she approached, though, her walk, her posture, her graceful demeanor looked so very familiar. When she drew closer to us, and I realized who it was, my heart skipped a beat. It was Jody, the girl I'd asked him about at the tennis courts. I wondered why he hadn't said anything, then I recalled his sour look when I'd mentioned her, and his tossing perfectly good tennis balls into the trash can.

"Hello, Carlos." She stepped into the dim flicker of the little citronella candle on the picnic table, but she looked at me, not him.

I did not know what to do. Stand? Smile? Shake hands? Salute?

"Who's your friend?" She continued to address Carlos, but did not take her eyes off me.

Carlos said something, but he wasn't there. All the energy was between me and Jody. I felt as if I were in an acting school improvisation where the instructor has set the scene: "You unexpectedly meet a former lover, one you still have strong feelings for; deal with it."

Jody and I dealt, and Carlos sat out the hand. He mumbled something about beer and ambled off into the house. I, a poor method-actor in college dramatic productions, suddenly became Marlon Brando. My mind whipped into the past and touched upon all of the sordid emotions that could prepare me for such a confrontation: I was a senior and she was a freshman. I graduated and went back to New York. I wanted to keep it going but, when I called, the Southern operators with their marshmallowed sweet-potato voices made South Carolina seem so far away from East Sixty-third Street.

Sometimes she averted her eyes, but they always came back to me. She was a nervous girl, who could have summoned great energy for acting, but would have lost her lunch each time she had to go on stage. Her long, straight brown hair seemed as fragile as she and, in certain light, you could see right through her pale skin. She was slightly taller than I, which had occasionally made us both feel awkward, but her looks and manner were as lovely and simple as the architecture on Magnolia Street. Finally, I summoned the courage to deliver my first line, and turned good drama into comedy.

"Have a seat." I waved my hand across the table and toppled a catsup bottle.

"New York City boy at a picnic," she said in her soft drawl, and shook her head.

"I still don't know which end of the fried chicken to hold but I do know we've got some catching up to do." I righted the catsup bottle.

"Always a pun." She pursed her lips in the semilaugh that had always enchanted me. She was so different from Bonnie Weber, and from my wife, who were more forceful, or forward, and who could do things like run away with my kid and a horse trainer. She was no wimp, though. In fact, she was strong in her way—at times most resolute. It shouldn't have bothered me that she was visiting Carlos. Perhaps—I hoped—they had simply stayed friends after I left. We'd often double-dated with Carlos and his girlfriend of the moment. I could see him chasing Jody, or anyone for that matter, but I could not see them as lovers. She was so gentle and he was so coarse and, although he was very much Americanized, he was still a foreigner. I was sure that Jody's mother, who had disliked me for merely being a Yankee, would give Carlos a much tougher time. Southerners aren't exactly xenophobic, but they do draw lines.

Suddenly Carlos came back with three cans of beer and a big grin on his face. Our improvisational scene was shattered, and I was relieved that the pressure was off. We chatted amiably for a while about current, impersonal matters, but it soon became obvious that I was the fifth wheel. I thanked Carlos for the dinner, and told Jody it was nice to see her again, and drove back to my rooming house.

Loneliness overwhelmed me as I pulled up in front of 22 Magnolia Street. I turned the engine off and sat a moment in the dark, and realized that the Garcias were not the foreigners. I was. They'd made me feel at home, though, at least until Jody walked in. For the first time in a long time, I wondered how long she had waited for me after I left her. I wondered if she had cried. I wondered how the walls of time and distance had affected her, and if she and Carlos stood together behind one wall and I behind another.

I got out of my Tempest and walked toward Mrs. Carswell's house. As I neared the side entrance, I looked up and saw that the light was on in the kitchen. My spirits rose to think that there might be someone up there, even Cowpens Martin. I needed a friend.

$\triangledown$

Chapter 6

COWPENS MARTIN WAS DRUNK in Mrs. Carswell's upstairs kitchen. He slurred some unintelligible greeting when I reached the top of the stairs. In my lonely state I was pleased to see him, and I smiled as he rummaged in a large brown paper bag, drew out a warm can of Budweiser, and set it before me on the kitchen table.

"Plenty more in this here paper poke." He nodded for me to take it.

I popped it open and downed half of it right away. I was surprised to be so thirsty after the long evening with Carlos, and so many beers. I was still sober, though, so I finished it off.

"Let's me and yew git drunk, prefesser." He handed me another, and I sat down with him.

"Looks like you've got a head start."

"I bin settin' here sippin' 'em all day, waitin' fer Warren."

"Oh, yes, Warren. . . ."

"College kids call 'im 'Warren the Queer,'" he said, and quickly added, "But I ain't of his persuasion, yew understand."

"Of course."

"And I don't chase no gals now, neither. Gettin' too old fer that."

"I think I am too," I said somewhat modestly, but truthfully all the same.

"Yer funnin' me, ain't yew, Jim?"

I was about to answer, but he immediately dismissed any notion he might have had that I could not cut the mustard, and went on about his friend Warren.

"Me and him jest talk, mostly . . . and about once a month we take a ride in that little pink T'bird, jest to keep her runnin'. Don't drive no more, though. Ain't even got no car."

"How do you get to work?"

He weaved on his chair a little and then sat up straight, seeming startled by such a practical consideration.

"Road crew truck swings by," he answered, "'bout six a.m. Flag wavin's an important job, yew know."

I tried to get a word in edgewise, but he was on a roll.

"Sometimes, after a good day's work, they drop me off at Elmer's Lounge and I drink a few. I'll drink a beer, you know, Jim."

He chugged another. My own pace, compared with his, slowed to a crawl. I was simply getting full. He kept on talking, and the evening was turning into a long, fuzzy night. I became concerned about getting to bed, and getting up for my Monday morning freshman English class. I was sure that Cowpens couldn't make the six a.m. road-crew truck, as he was nearly shellacked. I was about to go to my room, when I heard the door open downstairs.

"It's Warren!" He sat bolt upright, as though he were perfectly sober.

"Sure enough," a soft man's voice called out from the stairwell below.

Cowpens's eyes rolled up into his head as though he meditated on Sri Chinmoy, or as though he needed an oculist. Then a chubby little man arrived at the top of the stairs and stepped into the kitchen. Dramatically, he placed his hands on his womanish hips and asked in the bitchy tone that I'd heard so often from his type in New York, "Just who were you expecting?"

"That's 'whom'." Cowpens weaved precariously on his chair and I was amazed that he didn't topple, and that he had such concern for the English language.

"And we got an English prefesser right here to ast," he added.

"Where on earth did you find him?" Warren winked at me and minced his way to the kitchen table.

"Never yew mind that kinda talk," Cowpens scolded. "This here's Jim Harrington, a new boarder, and he's with the college."

Warren smiled prissily and offered his hand, palm down in that limp, effeminate gesture that had always annoyed me.

"Enchante," he said affectedly as we shook.

"And don't be speakin' none of that I-talian, neither."

"It's French," Warren lisped.

"Whatever, then. Stick to English. Jim's an English prefesser. Ain't that right, Jim?"

I looked at Warren under the glare of the bare hundred-watt bulb over Mrs. Carswell's kitchen table. He was built like a bowling pin, stoop-shouldered, large-hipped and squat, and everything about him was soft. He pulled out an extra chair and plopped down at the table with us.

Cowpens reached into his bag and pulled out a beer for his friend. He weaved at such an angle that I was ready to catch him before he hit the floor, but he miraculously defied gravity, as so many drunks can do, and sat straight up again to watch while Warren popped open the beer.

"Know it right here and now, Warren," he announced.

"Jim ain't interested in no fiddle-faddle, 'ceptin' with the opposite sex."

Comically, Warren raised his eyebrows and shot back, "Well, I'm opposite him at this table, and I can give him sex if he wants." He winked at me again to indicate he was only teasing. Cowpens became flustered, and Warren gave him some more.

"You know what they say: If you play in a bush, you'll swing on a limb."

I smiled at the wordplay, but Cowpens was indignant. "Yew jest concentrate on that tall boy I dun gave yew."

"Oooh, is Jim tall?" Sensing that I could appreciate the humor, he playfully motioned for me to stand up.

"Yew ole faggot, yew'd suck off the tailpipe of the Sutherland city bus."

"You old rednecks think everybody's chasing you."

They exchanged dire insults, as only the best of friends can do without consequence, but there was a high degree of tension. Cowpens was most concerned that he'd run off to New York with strangers, since he'd been beaten and robbed before, and there was now the fear of A.I.D.S. He glared at Warren, who tried to slough it off and make small talk with me.

"New York's my hometown," I threw out, trying for some relief.

"It's lovely," Warren offered, "and there's so very much to do."

"Yer always talkin' 'bout that danged city . . . but how come yew still live in Sutherland?" Cowpens challenged.

"Hush," Warren said softly. "I was born here. Besides, who would take care of you?"

"I got friends." Cowpens slobbered and swilled more beer. "Jim's muh friend, ain't yew?"

"Of course," I said quickly, and before he could speak again, led the conversation back to Warren.

"What do you do?" I asked.

"I work at Price's, the men's clothing store on Main Street."

I brightened. "I know them. I shopped there when I was an undergraduate."

I noticed that Warren, aside from appearing in need of a shower and shave from his impulsive, luggageless trip to New York, looked somewhat natty in an expensive though rumpled pair of trousers and a fine silk shirt.

"I never bought much, though. They were always a little pricey for me," I said.

"I'm sure you can afford us, now that you're a wealthy professor." He ignored my pun and looked at Cowpens, whose eyes were shut, on the verge of sleep or passing out. Then he looked back at me and said, "Since we're all such good friends, perhaps I'll give you a discount when you come in."

It was unfair, but I envisioned his delight at measuring the inseams of his clientele.

"I'm not much for clothes." I shrugged off the invitation and then realized I'd given him an opening to appraise me with the smug expertise of a couturier and haughtily pronounce, "That's obvious." But he only declared, without the slightest trace of sarcasm, or effeminateness, that he wasn't much into clothes either.

"I just get these duds cheaper than I can buy work clothes at Sears." He hooked a well-manicured thumb under the lapel of his silk shirt.

At first I was wary of his sudden modesty, which could have been a ploy to gain my trust and loosen me for a sexual overture. Then I scolded myself for thinking like so many men who, insecure in their own masculinity, fear men like Warren. And gay men must laugh at those who are vain and arrogant enough to think they're irresistible. I'd known men who were physically attracted to me, and found that if I treated them as I would any other individual, there was never a blatant come-on. And the conversation was generally far more interesting than that available with some macho man who believes that the dissolution of barriers and a meeting of the minds can only lead to sex. So I took Warren's comment about his clothes at face value, and believed he was only being friendly. We talked while Cowpens weaved nearly unconscious on his chair, though he occasionally opened his eyes and loudly echoed something we said.

"He's a good man," Warren told me. "He just drinks too much."

"The college kids treat him poorly, down at Elmer's Tradewinds Lounge." The memory of Cowpens lying under that pinball machine was all too vivid.

"I've had to go get him out of there." He shook his head and looked fondly, almost maternally, at his sleepy friend.

"One thing struck me as odd," I ventured.

"What's that?" He raised his eyebrows.

"Elmer caters only to the college crowd. Why does he let Cowpens in?"

He laughed softly, and then sipped his beer and scowled. "This is so warm."

Deciding not to drink any more, I pushed the remainder of my nearly full can aside.

"It's quite a story," Warren continued. "Not only does Elmer let him in, but he drinks free . . . for life."

"Free drinks!" Cowpens shouted. He sat up straight, and looked at his beer as though ready to drink, but slowly leaned back again and let his eyes shut.

"You're kidding," I said softly to Warren.

"Elmer's wasn't always a college boy's bar, you know. Originally, it was a redneck poolroom and bar, with huge jars of pickled eggs, pig's feet, Slim Jims, a few skody old whores and a Rock-Ola that only played Buck Owens. The men from the cotton mills went there, the lintheads, the loom tenders, only the crackers . . . and Cowpens."

He paused and took another sip of his beer, and scowled again at its warmth.

"One night, years ago, Cowpens was in there shooting pool with a bunch of the good ole boys. He worked at the cotton mill then, Yates Sutherland's. I'm sure you know him."

"He was a classmate of mine."

"Too bad." He pouted. "I don't mean that as derogatory, exactly, but he does come in to buy clothes from time to time."

Considering the ridiculous puce smoking jacket Yates had worn at the party, I was not sure if Warren meant he was a real pain in the neck as a customer, or if he referred to his extremely poor taste in clothing. I did not pursue it, though, since I was more curious about Cowpens.

"Anyway," he continued, "a man came into Elmer's and pulled a gun. He pointed it at Elmer and demanded all the cash in the register. He said he'd kill him if he didn't give it over." He paused and looked off across the room, as though picturing the event in his mind.

"What happened?" I pressed.

"Oh. Elmer froze. It looked as though he couldn't move, and the gunman would surely blast him. I wasn't there, you know. Cowpens told me, the only time he's ever talked about it."

He looked again at his friend, and I'm not sure he would

have continued the story had I not egged him on.

"Please excuse me," he said. "I know I've made you curious. It happened that Cowpens put down his pool stick and stepped directly between Elmer and that crazed killer. I'm not sure he was drunk at the time, but it's a good possibility, since he looked the man directly in the eyes and said, just as calmly as you please, 'You better hope that gun's chocolate, 'cause you're gonna eat it.' The newspaper printed that. It's a fact."

"Truth in journalism." I'd meant the comment to be general, that I didn't believe everything I read in newspapers, but Warren picked up on it and, lucky for me, became more earnest than indignant.

"You wouldn't believe it to look at him, but others have confirmed it," he said.

"I believe you," I said earnestly, with a look that told him to go on.

"Well, he raised the gun, stuck it right up to Cowpens's forehead, and cocked back the hammer. And our friend here just stared at him and didn't move, and repeated, 'You're gonna eat it.'"

I grimaced and wondered how that broken, scrawny little man could have mustered that kind of courage.

"But you can see there's no hole in his forehead. The man simply could not accept the challenge. He stepped back, smiled, stuck the gun in his own mouth, and blew the back of his head off."

I grimaced again, and he must have mistaken my look of horror for incredulity.

"It's true. I saw the newspaper article, and Elmer doesn't give away many free beers."

"I believe that, but I wouldn't have faced that loaded gun for all the drinks in the world."

"Drinks!" Cowpens suddenly pitched forward and, before either of us could catch him, his head thudded on the kitchen table. He remained there, passed out cold. We both winced at the sound, but he at least looked more comfortable than he had trying to sit up in his chair.

"He was brave, or foolhardy, once," Warren said, "but now he needs someone to care for him."

I asked if we should take him to his room, but Warren insisted he'd only wake up and get mad. I yawned and realized I was ready to go to my room, but his next statement held me.

"I went to Sutherland College, you know. I was kicked out before the end of the first semester. The dean of students himself caught me in bed with another boy. I think the old pervert got his rocks off barging into young boys' rooms, ostensibly to check for liquor and such, but hoping to catch them fresh out of the shower. That was a long time ago, though. Today, I wouldn't even be sent to the school psychologist. In fact, I might be applauded if I said I'd turned down the heat to conserve energy and popped into the sack with my roomie to keep warm."

He smiled slyly, almost flirtatiously, but it was only his manner, not a come-on. I felt sorry for him and asked if they would have let him come back.

"I could have," he said, "after a probationary period. But my father withdrew his support of my education, and then of me. He eventually left Sutherland and moved down to Columbia. I'd embarrassed him. He was a dentist here, and highly visible."

"Too bad you weren't in New York."

"What can I tell you. You know the South. . . ."

He yawned and stretched, and I hoped he was tired and I could escape. I feared that the dreariness of those two companions would only sink me lower. I saw my life linked with theirs, and all of my mistakes and misunderstandings glared harsher than Mrs. Carswell's bare hundred-watt bulb.

Warren spoke on, but I couldn't hear him. I could only see my wife with that horse trainer. I wondered if she was bored, and if she had realized the error of her ways. But as low as I was, I could never go back there, to live in her periphery and scrounge for my moments as a father, while she grudgingly gave up the child, or gleefully had me serve as a baby-sitter while she and her latest lover escaped for an unencumbered weekend. Even if she begged me, I couldn't go back, as much as I loved the Northeast and longed to be there. In my undergraduate days I occasionally drove out to the interstate highway just to look north. I'd followed that road so many times in my mind's eye, and ticked off the major cities along the way: Charlotte, Richmond, Washington, Baltimore, and Philadelphia. I cheered on summer trips home when I reached the sign on the New Jersey Turnpike that read *New York 100 miles*. Then I'd hit the special button on the car radio, and the strong pulse of WABC-AM would suck me in. Ah, reentry. The retro-rockets had worked. I had gone to the ends of the universe and returned, running at impossible speeds under Spanish moss, through kudzu and across swamps. . . .

Warren was still talking, wrecking my journey, bringing me back to the South and the tiny wrinkles in his baby-soft skin. I wondered if he'd had a face peel. Then I wondered why he'd stayed at the scene of his crime, and hadn't gone to lose himself in some more understanding place like New Orleans or Atlanta. I asked him that, in what I regretfully realized was an annoyed tone of voice.

"I like it here," he answered simply. "And occasionally, though it's becoming very rare, I get to climb into the sack with a pretty college boy."

"I suppose. . . ." I was about to excuse his sexual predilection, but he stopped me from being a fool.

"Also, I had no money," he said. "I had to work . . . and I didn't do anything wrong."

I respected the fact that he had not fled, as I had, and I wished I could be as honest. For when he asked me why I had come back to my old alma mater, I handed him some quick mumbo jumbo about being on a sabbatical to learn more about the South than I had in my four short undergraduate years.

"And I know one thing." I stood and yawned, ready to excuse myself. "I can't stay up all night and make those early classes like I could in the old days."

"I'll drink to that." He stood and swallowed the remainder of his beer.

"And how's he going to be ready for the road crew when they swing by tomorrow morning?" I looked down at Cowpens, who hadn't stirred.

"Oh, he'll make it." Warren chuckled.

"I won't be able to when I'm fifty-two."

"Is that what he told you? Why, that old devil. He's sixty-two if he's a day."

"I wondered. . . ."

"Even he doesn't know. There were no records of his birth where he came from, and his folks died when he was young. Another family took him in only because he was just old enough to help work their farm, and could produce more than he could eat. This is a poor state, as you know, Jim."

$\triangledown$

Chapter 7

MONDAY MORNING, BONNIE WEBER. Front row, center, green eyes wide, wearing the same smile she'd had on in my car after Yates Sutherland's party Saturday night. I felt naked before her on the lectern, and I kept hearing her raunchy stripper's song, which would certainly outdo my lecture on the bawdiness of Chaucer. Tentatively, I opened the textbook and turned to "The Miller's Tale." I'd planned to reveal the libertinism therein, to corrupt and shock them, to hit them with the raunch that their delicate, television-nurtured minds were now entitled to know. I'd planned to fill their bowdlerized brains with the Wife of Bath's grubby scatology. But all that paled as Bonnie's eyes devoured me, and I realized those kids already knew much more than I. So, pretending to search in the text for my place to start, I was pricked with an untoward sense of modesty and glanced down to see if my fly was open.

My lecture bored them. I lost even the football players, who still elbowed one another like big playful bears at the back of the room, but who paid me little attention. They'd abandoned their defensive wall of support for my weak jokes, as though I were a quarterback they hated, as though they missed their blocks on purpose so I would get blitzed. Under such pressure, I feebly threw my bomb. It was Chaucer's line about the knight "pricking" (Middle English for "riding") on the plain. It fell flat. Playboy had better jokes. Penthouse left nothing to the imagination. I'd gotten titters at least for that line in Saratoga Springs, but that was an all-girl's school, and that was before Bonnie Weber. I struggled to finish the lecture and, when the period ended, retaliated for my ineptitude by hitting them with a whopping assignment. The class filed out, mumbling their discontent, but Bonnie lingered.

"I enjoyed the lecture, professor."

"I was groping," I said matter-of-factly. "Nothing came together."

I collected my notes from the lectern and stuffed them between the pages of the *Norton's Anthology* that was my briefcase.

"No, it gelled," she insisted. "You make Chaucer fun."

"Flattery won't improve your grade, Miss Weber." I tucked the fat little book under my arm and turned to go. I was brusque on purpose. Though I found her very attractive, I did not want her to go too far, to become too familiar and to tempt me anymore. The risks were too great, I had decided. But she was not one to be put off.

"I'll grade you, professor." Her green eyes sparkled.

"You said that in my car the other night, and it got you excused."

"About that." She took on a look of concern. "I didn't mean to come on so strong. I apologize. I'd had too much wine."

She was so earnest that I was compelled to try to forget the whole incident, and I regretted that I had been so cold.

"Come on," I said as a few students wandered in for the next class, which wasn't mine. "I've got an hour break. I'll buy us coffee at the canteen."

"I really should go and start the hundred pages you assigned us for Wednesday," she told me as she walked to the door.

"Okay." I shrugged, realizing she'd turned the tables on me.

"Actually, I have another class." She smiled and all the positive sexual tension between us returned. Then the bell rang again and she darted off down the hall. I watched her run, skirt taut across her shapely hips and firm rear end. I could not comprehend her womanliness, in spite of her youth. She seemed so in command of any situation. Her aggressiveness bothered me, though. It was a trait I found less than admirable. And I seemed to lump such women into one category: fast, good time but no hope for anything lasting. I'm sure that's unfair, based on my own insecurity and inadequacy. Anyway, I had been drunk at Yates Sutherland's party, and had probably sent signals I shouldn't have.

I walked alone to the college canteen for some coffee during my hour break. I was tired from the long night before with Cowpens and Warren, and was relieved to be out of their desolate sphere for the moment, to reestablish my niche in the world of higher education. I drank in the Sutherland College campus, which was thick with so many outstandingly large magnolias, and enough variety in other genuses so the botany department seldom left the grounds for field study. I appreciated what had been done to preserve and restore the old buildings, and the new structures, though modern in style, for the most part blended tastefully with the historic. Except for the music building, the newest on campus and the only one that was shamelessly out of place. It was pointy, with angular spires and protuberances that clashed with the Southern Simple architecture and lush magnolias. I was told that Mrs. Sutherland herself had designed it, though I could have guessed. Like her home, it was cacophonous and piercing.

I reached the canteen, which was adjacent to the new dining hall, both part of a modern dormitory complex that had been completed the previous summer. Inside, I was impressed by the canteen's spiffy new interior and its large plate-glass windows that looked across the campus toward Old Main. I stepped up to the food service counter and asked for coffee and a bagel, but the woman behind the counter gave me such a quizzical look that I shifted my order to a glazed doughnut without trying to explain.

I sat at a small table behind a stand for sugar, stirrers, packets of mustard, and such, where I could hide as though in a duck blind and watch the wildlife. Some students were ordering grilled pimento-cheese sandwiches for breakfast, and I wondered what kind of a look they'd get from a deli counter-man in New York for that. Then one of them ordered a bottle of Pepsi and a packet of salted peanuts, and carefully funneled the nuts into the bottle, shook it, and drank. I had not seen that practice since I was an undergraduate, and I was pleased to see the quaint habit had not died out in the wake of the New South. I enjoyed hearing their Southern drawls, and thought they'd be surprised to know how much influence they'd had on New York-ese, from pre-Civil War days when cotton traders came up the coast on barges and ships.

Suddenly, a husky voice interrupted my study of Southern accents and gustatory delights. Bonnie Weber's contralto had found me behind my duck blind, and it turned every head in the room.

"Hello, Jim-except-in-class."

"Pretend we're in class." I was conscious of the students watching me now.

"Okay, professor." She smiled, undaunted, and sat at my table.

"I thought you had a class."

"I cut it. Music Appreciation. Mrs. Sutherland."

"That's important."

"It's a guaranteed A. Unlike you, professor, she thinks I'm talented."

I smiled, and lightened up, and offered to buy her some coffee. When she said she'd take a Pepsi instead, I raised an eyebrow.

"Caffeine and sugar come in many forms," she told me.

"Want some peanuts to pour down the neck?" We laughed together, Yankees in the rebel encampment. I bought her a Pepsi, in a bottle, and another coffee for me. On the way back to the table, I noticed more youngsters filing into the canteen. Bonnie fit in with them so well; I saw that I was no longer part of the Pepsi generation. My mind bounced between her excellent operatics at the Sutherland's party and her stripper's song in the front seat of my car, and I decided to lecture her a little more.

"Don't forget"—I handed her the Pepsi—"this is the last class I want you to miss."

"Do you ever go out, professor?" She ignored my admonishment and brought the bottle provocatively to her full lips.

"Not with my students. People like Yates Sutherland frown on that, and they always find out."

"Who cares what that old fart thinks?"

"Hey! That old fart happens to be my age."

"There's no comparing you two, professor. And I don't mean a real date. I mean like go out to the local pub and talk with your students."

She was clever. I admired that. She blew a mellow note across the mouth of the Pepsi bottle, with a look that made me laugh.

"Pub, you said? I don't think there's anything like a pub in Sutherland."

"There's Elmer's Tradewinds."

"That's a dump." I scowled, thinking of Cowpens Martin lying under that pinball machine.

"But it's the only place within walking distance, and we're only freshman, without cars."

She had me. I liked to meet with groups of my students outside of class, on the campus or off somewhere in a bar. It was a relief for me and for them. In a relaxed atmosphere, they could come back at me more easily about something I'd said in the heat of a lecture. They could teach me and remind me that the teacher is just an extension of the student. I'd have to be careful, though, since meeting her alone at Elmer's would be tantamount to a date, whether we were discussing Chaucer or trying to charm the pants off each other.

"And there will be other students there?"

"Of course. Tonight. Come on, professor."

I agreed to go, and she promised not to cut any more classes on purpose.

That afternoon, when my classes were finished, I went to the bursar's office. Yates Sutherland had informed me that I would be coaching the tennis team, whether I wanted to or not, but that he'd pay me in advance. I didn't argue. Repairs to my Tempest would be expensive, and my money was so low that I was worried about being able to pay for my own drinks at Elmer's Tradewinds with Bonnie and the other students that night. Anyway, coaching could be fun. I thought about holding a few fall practices—my option—but then I considered the long series of home matches and road trips next spring. I would have to travel to them all, and baby-sit for what would probably be a losing team, rueing the fact that Sutherland was such a small private college with so bare a minimum of athletic talent to go around and scholarships allotted only to football.

I took the little check with too few numbers on it and, as I left the bursar's office, tried to lift my spirits by recalling the fun I'd had with the craziness and enthusiasm that came from strictly volunteer sport in my undergraduate days. I walked over to the old tennis courts, and saw that they were as dilapidated as ever, with torn nets, faded lines, and cracked tarmac, but I smiled to recall our distinct home-court advantage. We knew all the cracks and gullies by heart, and aimed for them in practice to perfect the infamous and unreturnable "Sutherland Bounce" that drove visiting teams to distraction. Occasionally, however, it drove us nuts, too. One visiting team took pictures of me climbing a courtside tree to retrieve my racquet, which I'd heaved over the fence in disgust when it seemed my opponent had perfected hitting our trenches and slick spots better than I.

Two girls came out to play and I watched them for a few moments. They were terrible, but when they bent to pick up a ball their scanty nylon running shorts rode up on their buttocks and made quite a display. They looked so young, most likely freshmen, probably twenty years my junior. If I had entertained any thoughts about having an affair with Bonnie Weber, watching those young girls hit the ball made me think again. I could have been their father and, if I indulged myself, it would only shove me further down into the sleazy sphere of the likes of Cowpens Martin. Then I thought of something Cowpens had said in Mrs. Carswell's kitchen, in our chewing the fat and solving most of the major problems of the world. Somehow we'd touched on the subject of young college girls. I'd said, perhaps trying to be manly and declare that I wasn't bait for "Warren the Queer," that young girls could be "amusing," and except for a wink, and perhaps a sly smile, I'd left it at that. But Cowpens sensed that I wasn't so macho and astutely intimated that I wasn't really interested in using someone half my age for sex. Though I can't recall his exact words, he told me such a young lady might look to me for acceptance, and I could only do her damage if I rebuffed her. He said that I could teach her, most likely better than most, where a boy her own age might mistreat her and take her for granted. I could, with proper handling, he told me, make her strong. "But," he concluded, "young er old, prefesser, they all end up handlin' yew."

I left the tennis courts and headed for my car, past groups of students hurrying between classes. I felt old and professorly in their wake. They moved as if in a strobe effect; here a boy darting among companions and flicking gestures, there a girl tossing her head in laughter, hair electric in the breeze. Their energy dazzled, and Bonnie Weber belonged with them, not with me.

She and her friends did not show up that night at Elmer's Tradewinds. Instead, to my amazement, Jody walked in . . . and I saw Cowpens Martin alive for the last time.

$\triangledown$

Chapter 8

ELMER RECOGNIZED ME AS I stepped under the Schlitz globe at the bar of the Tradewinds Lounge.

"Don't tell me," he said. "Bottle of Bud . . . fart in a bathtub . . . right, pardner?"

"That's droll, Elmer."

"Huh?"

"Oh, nothing. . . ."

"I hearda that 'droll.' It's one of them fancy German beers, right? We don't carry it though."

I considered enlightening him as to Cowpens Martin's special word, but decided to let him stew because he didn't stock any "droll." So I smirked and told him that a Budweiser would have to do, and he smiled sheepishly and went off to get one for me. While my eyes adjusted to the dim light, I looked around and was surprised to find that the place was empty. Monday night had never slaked my thirst in school and I squinted into some of the darker corners, certain that Bonnie and her friends were there. But it was just me and Elmer, and the pinball machine, which was oddly silent under its halo of colored lights. At least I was pleased to see that Cowpens was not underneath it. It would be awkward to explain to my students that I lived with the old redneck. . . .

"Say, I'd be happy to order a case of that there 'droll,' if you'd write down how you spell it," Elmer said as he returned with my Bud.

I took a few quick swallows and then declined his offer. I hoped he'd go away and wash glasses or something off at the other end of the bar, but he stayed with me under that Schlitz globe and grinned.

"Where are the customers?" I asked more to needle him than because I was curious, or worried that Bonnie might not come.

"Happens, pardner." He tried to act nonchalant, but I caught him looking at my bottle to see if it was empty. The fact that it was nearly full discouraged him more than any words I could muster, so I got my wish and he wandered away to the other end of the bar.

I waited until eleven, and, to Elmer's chagrin, nursed only two more beers the whole time. I was more relieved than annoyed that nobody had showed up. It's tough to be prepared for students at all hours, early in the morning, late at night. Their enthusiasm is so strong and unflagging, and they can never understand how you might tire of answering their questions. You can never tell them that you love their brightness and their inspiration but you're not too fond of Walt Whitman anymore. So, longing for the quiet streets of Sutherland and my cozy little niche at Mrs. Carswell's, Cowpens and Warren notwithstanding, I paid Elmer and started for the door.

As I turned to leave, I saw Jody standing there, just in the door way—an apparition amazingly conjured up from the quiet streets. She had not yet seen me and her eyes went first to the bar, to the Schlitz globe and the grinning Elmer, from where I'd stepped into the gloom. She walked in a little more, tentative as a careful kitten, and then stopped. My heart stopped too, and my mind raced through a thousand reasons why she might be there. Was she looking for Carlos? No. He only frequented the glitter sports, the Holiday Inn or the Ramada, with their elaborate decor and live entertainment, which drew the movers and shakers in from Interstate 85. Then she saw me. She smiled shyly and came forward, looking so out of place. Bonnie would have strutted in, and her wake would have torn the fluorescent posters off the walls. Jody felt her way in, each step an excursion, a painful trek that at least equaled the distance from Sutherland to New York.

"How did you know. . . ." I was flustered. We'd been lovers so long ago, and so much had changed, but so much had not.

"I drove by 22 Magnolia," she said softly, "and your car wasn't there. I cruised by the campus and didn't see you. I even went by Carlos's house, but I didn't stop in."

"I'm glad."

"You don't have to say that."

"I mean, I'm glad you didn't stop in to see Carlos."

"How can you say that?"

"I mean. . . ." I was stumped. I certainly had no right to be jealous. I was being stupid and if I didn't calm down, everything I said would be a blunder.

"How did you know I live at 22 Magnolia?" I asked, trying to start the conversation over.

"I have my ways." She pursed her lips into the sweet, wry smile that I always remembered. They were full lips, fuller than Bonnie's, but her soft, Southern voice was nowhere near as deep.

"Carlos says that a lot."

"I have my ways?"

I nodded, annoyed that I had brought up Carlos again.

"You pick up a few phrases when you hang around

someone," she said evenly, but I knew it was a signal to shut up about Carlos.

To Elmer's delight, I bought drinks for us and ushered her to a table in the darkest corner I could find. If Bonnie came in, I hoped she might take a quick look around, figure the place was empty, and leave.

I was glad to sit, since I'd stood at the bar all night, and since I was more comfortable talking with Jody when we were seated; she was at least an inch taller than I. She was also slender, almost too thin, a contrast to Bonnie, and my wife, who were sturdy, low-slung, and built for comfort. Jody had boy's hips, long legs, and a narrow upper torso that made her ample breasts seem extra large. I liked that; it was most erotic. Recalling her naked body on my bed so many years ago, I forgot it was my turn to talk.

"You there?"

"Sorry. . . . I was just thinking."

"What about?"

"Us."

"You don't have to say that."

I looked into her eyes, but she looked down and then away. It was obvious, in spite of the fact that she'd come to me, that our relationship could not be as easily rekindled as that of old tennis buddies going out on the court again. Then I wondered why Carlos had brought me back to his home, and why he'd even played tennis with me.

"Can we see each other?"

"We're seeing each other now."

I was pleased that she needled me. She'd always had a good sense of humor, and it was nice to think that some of the old familiarity was still there.

"What I mean," I said, "is how serious are you with . . . you know who."

"Carlos?" she looked as though we'd never mentioned the name before. "Oh, him. You know what he's like."

"I know, but he's my friend, and there's honor among thieves."

"What do you mean by that?"

"It's just an expression. What I really mean is, how long have you been seeing him?"

"A while." She looked down again and, with one finger, traced a design in the moisture on the outside of her glass.

"That tells me a lot."

"Pretty long, then."

"How long?"

"Off and on . . . since you left."

"Sixteen years!"

"I said off and on."

"My God. You're practically married to the guy."

"You're the only one who's married." She looked me in the eye. "And heaven knows I should never be seen in a place like this with a married man."

She kept a straight face for a moment but, to my great relief, let loose a smile and then a laugh. We both laughed. She could play the proper Southern damsel with aplomb.

"Why did you stay?" I asked her. "I thought you hated Sutherland."

"I had no place to go."

"And you wanted to be near Carlos?"

She paused a moment, and I expected a reprimand for mentioning his name again, but with a faint smile she answered my question from her heart.

"He was you . . . or all that was left of you."

Suddenly the memories became all too vivid. The reality set in. She was no longer the Patient Griselda, the fair damsel who had waited so faithfully and so long for her night to come home from the Crusades. She was real, and she'd adjusted, as would anyone with any common sense.

"We both dated others, of course."

"Of course. . . ." I tried to act nonchalant, as Elmer had earlier about the lack of customers, but her comment did nothing to comfort me.

"I'm not in love with him." She had read my thoughts.

"But if he loves you, and we see each other, he'll think I wrecked it."

"There's nothing to wreck, except . . . " She paused, considering something.

"Except what?"

"Well . . . he did ask me to marry him . . . once."

"You mean one time, or once upon a time?"

"Last night, after you left."

My jaw dropped, though her offhand manner told me what her answer had been. She smiled again, and I saw that same coy, girlish look that had enchanted me when she was a freshman, when she was so tender and new to the big college town from rural Ninety-six, South Carolina.

"And you told him . . . "

"I said I'd think on it," she drawled, consciously like Scarlet O'Hara.

"You should have said no, if you don't love him." I played the practical Yankee, but she proved far more practical.

"I haven't had any better offers," she said, "and I'm not getting any younger."

"I couldn't ask you," I scoffed. "I'm not even divorced yet." I'd meant it half as a joke, then regretted saying it.

"You?" She raised her eyebrows. "You're entirely too unstable."

"You're too right. But would you hold off with Carlos, on the basis of seeing me again?" I had to make a play, or maybe lose her forever. She had taken the initiative, and I had to follow up. Her allure was still too strong, my memories of our love too fond. I had never really stopped thinking of her strange sweetness, of her slow talk and sultriness—my best recollections of college and the South. I had to balance the act, though, to be sure I was not resurrecting a dead, long-abandoned love merely because I had lost everything.

Jody had stayed in Sutherland after graduating from the college, and had taken a job teaching Latin at Sutherland High School. She'd achieved a certain independence, but her family in nearby Ninety-six kept a close watch on her. I recalled that her parents had always been wary guilt-instillers. The few times I had met them had not been pleasant. Her father was a Ku Klux Klan member, I was certain. He was a tractor salesman, with a row of pens always straining his breast pocket, hair trimmed short, shaved, and spiffy. And as he was the archetypal solid Southern businessman, Jody's mother was the model of a Southern belle: a slow-talking, sloe-eyed witch who knew all the dirt in Ninety-six and in many surrounding counties. Like her daughter, she had a strong, underlying sensuality, though it was hard to imagine that her husband was capable of unleashing that quality. He was too stiff, too much the bluenose, the solid pillar of the local Methodist Church, ever to reverse the missionary posture accepted in Ninety-six.

I had it all figured out, at least that's how it seemed to me when I was a college senior and thought I knew everything. I thought I knew Jody then. I thought she was as Southern Simple as the architecture on Magnolia Street, and I couldn't see behind that facade. I couldn't see how strong she was, how clever, how brave. Her skin was so pale and delicate, so prone to attacks of shingles every time we fought and I failed to call. There was no hint of how well she was buttressed within, how rooted she was in the Southern psyche—in the red clay and bedrock agrarian foundation that held it all together behind the self-erected concealment of sluggishness, of molasses in January, and the fable that your IQ automatically drops ten points when you live below the Mason-Dixon line. And it hit me strongly, so many years later in the dim light of Elmer's Tradewinds Lounge, that both Jody and the South, in spite of war wounds and scars, had remained individuals, vestiges of the never-vanquished Confederacy.

Entrenched as she was, I marveled at how far she could wander, how she could escape the red clay of the Carolinas and Georgia and take us both back to the very beginning of the civilized world. There, she'd whispered to me in Latin from the love poems of Catullus. And I, lost in passion, had needed no translation. The message was in her long, petal-soft fingers as she trembled on the verge of abandon but somehow clung to the meter of her carnal song, declining "amo . . . amas . . . amat" . . . teasing me with warm visions of the Isle of Lesbos . . . making me wonder at her Sapphic serenade. We'd floated through the Green Isles, above sun-bleached ancient ruins, across the bluest seas with no wrecks, no sharks, and no bottom. . . .

Jody did not answer my question that night. Elmer broke the mood when he dropped a quarter into the jukebox and Pablo Cruse crooned, "When my baby smiles at me I go to Rio. . . ." In that instant, the perfectly blue Aegean turned into a festering sewer, and I could only think of Carlos sticking his calloused Gaucho's cock into Jody's precious love triangle. He was Othello on Desdemona, an old ram tupping my ewe, his sweaty balls bashing mercilessly against the tiny, puckered portal beneath her sweet mons. "Fuck her between the tits and shoot her in the throat," was Carlos's poetry. I'd heard him say it many times. Girls who spoke "on a hairy microphone" were his muse. That was his crude way of saying they'd orally service their dates. It was amusing then, when we were only tennis buddies and nothing was sacred. He even joked about the "umbrella treatment" for a venereal infection he'd once contracted. "They stick a tube in your dick, man, open it like a little umbrella and pull it out . . . Fiera puta, what pain!" Suddenly his comic Portuguese was nasty compared with Jody's sterile Latin . . . even compared with the ribaldry of Catullus. The spell was thoroughly broken and, leaving Jody to consider if she'd hold off with Carlos on the basis of seeing me again, I jumped up to go to the men's room. I smirked but said nothing to Elmer as I passed the bar, and he grinningly assured me that he'd order a case of that fancy German beer.

The men's room, a makeshift plywood construction at the rear of the lounge, held a toilet you wouldn't sit on and a sink you wouldn't touch, as it was often used as urinal on crowded nights. As I stood and went about my business, I could see out a small open window that looked onto Elmer's back lot. There was a trash container there, a large "Dempster Dumpster" crammed to overflowing with beer cans and cartons, a smelly shambles that reminded me of New York City during a garbage strike. But it was marginally better to look at than Elmer's piss-crusted sink and john, I thought, until the full moon, high and far away, came from behind a cloud and illuminated a huge rat that poked among the rubbish in the dumpster.

They used to shoot rats for sport in my undergraduate days, on long Saturday afternoons when there was nothing to do but go out to the city dump. The country boys pulled their squirrel guns from out of nowhere and the ROTC boys brought their M-14's, and they surrounded a steaming pile of garbage and blasted away. I went along once, because my roommate insisted, and used his gun to pump a few bullets into a nasty rat. Marveling at how we managed not to shoot one another, I vowed never to go back. Ironically, in that same year, a student was accidently shot in one of the dorms and then guns were forbidden on campus.

I zipped up my pants and tried to shift my thoughts from garbage, rats, and an American's God-given right to bear arms, back to Jody, but a strange sound made me look out the window at the dumpster again. Something had moved under the rubble that spilled over the side. It had to be bigger than a rat, probably a cat or a dog, I thought, as I stepped out of the men's room and stopped a moment by the open back door to the lounge. First I looked at the bar, and saw that Elmer was no longer behind it. He was at our table, talking with Jody, surely trying to sell her a bottle of Bud, probably telling her how it sounds like a fart in a bathtub or, for Latin teachers, "flatus in bathtubbum." Anyway, they did not notice me so I stepped outside the back door into the back lot by the dumpster, the rat ignored me, too involved in gnawing an old Slim Jim wrapper, too comfortable in what Elmer had let become a serious mess. The entire lot was crammed with rubbish, and the smell made it apparent that the dumpster had not been emptied in weeks. Either Elmer was a pig, or business was so bad that he couldn't pay his carting bill.

Suddenly something big moved again under all the rubbish, and I heard a groan that was from no dog or cat. I looked down and saw a pointy boot, and the shock of recognition hit me in an instant. I'd seen that battered and scuffed boot too many times before, and when it moved again I knew it hadn't been thrown out there, where it belonged. I knew it was still attached to the scrawny leg of Cowpens Martin. I quickly kicked some boxes away and then dropped to my knees and shoveled through more of the rubbish. The stench of stale beer filled my nose, and then I smelled blood. Cowpens lay on his back and struggled for breath. One side of his skull was a mess, hit often with something heavy. He could only open one eye, and he looked at me and grasped my wrist with his scrawny hand. He tried to talk, but I told him not to, that I'd go get help. I got up a little, but he held me. I was amazed at the strength of his grip.

"W-wu're . . . f-friend . . . " his speech was thick and slurred, like a record played at too slow a speed.

"We're friends, yes, so I'll get help," I said, but he wouldn't let go of my wrist.

"P-pink . . . car . . . "

"Warren's car?"

"T-tire. . . . Yours. . . ."

Finally his grip loosened and I ran inside, shouting for Elmer to call an ambulance. As if he didn't trust me, as though I played a college kid's prank, he first wandered hesitantly out back to see what had happened. Then he hurried to the phone and I went back to Cowpens, with Jody following.

I knelt by him again and whispered, "Who did it?" There was no answer. I felt for a pulse, but there was none. Luckily, Jody put her hand over her mouth and went away, and I gave him mouth-to-mouth breathing. No response. I pounded his chest. Still no pulse. I stood and looked at him. He seemed asleep, just as he had under the pinball machine, except for all the blood.

The police came quickly, followed closely by an ambulance. I told them I thought he was dead, but they paid me no attention and went to work. They soon gave up, however, and a big detective in a brown suit entered and began asking questions.

"Who found him?"

"I did."

"How?"

"I heard him when I was in the men's room."

"Then he was still alive."

"Barely."

"Did you see anyone else?"

"No."

"Did he say anything?"

"Just babble. Incoherent."

The detective looked at the ambulance men.

"He couldn't have talked much," one of them drawled, "not with his head mashed in like that."

The detective took Jody and me aside and asked more questions. The fact that I was a college professor, with Jody there and Elmer looking on, should have put me completely above suspicion, but the fact that Cowpens and I lived in the same rooming house made him very curious. I could see that Jody was surprised too, and I worried more about what she thought about my living with Cowpens than about being suspected of murder. The detective finally took a long, hard look at me and seemed to decide I didn't do it.

Jody and I were released, and Elmer was taken aside for more questions. Our reunion was wrecked and, having decided to go home, we walked together out to the street.

"Will I see you again?" I asked.

"Maybe." She smiled, I thought, but quickly got into her car and drove away before I could figure out her expression.

As I drove back to Mrs. Carswell's, I wondered why I hadn't told the detective Cowpens's exact last words, and decided to take a look at the spare tire of the pink T'bird.

$\triangledown$

Chapter 9

COME IN. THE SYNTHESIZER is Synthesizing. read a small sign on the door to John Hill's office. Known as "The Rock," Hill had occupied that little office, at the bottom of a stairwell in the basement of the oldest dormitory on campus, at least since he was my freshman geology professor, and probably aeons before. All time was geologic time to The Rock, and the building would erode to dust before he'd consider moving, though he was a senior member of the faculty and one of the most respected scholars within the institution and without. He'd published several books and hundreds of papers and could have moved wherever he wanted and taught at any school. But he stayed at Sutherland for the token payment of a dollar a year. He'd made a great deal of money, more than he needed, he said, as a petroleum geologist for one of the big oil companies. He was still retained as a consultant to find an oil field now and then, but he loved the life at Sutherland, the time to teach and study, and the freedom to ponder the great mysteries of the earth's formation. His enthusiasm for magma's molton message flowed to his students.

If The Rock had a fault, it was that he too often conferred the credit for "genius," when students blindly stumbled to a revelation with him holding their hand. He was like Howard Cosell, I thought, who ascribed genius to any 250-pound moron with a glimmer of insight for effective blocking in the interior line. Most remarkable to me, however, was that The Rock never locked his office door. His students were welcome to enter at any time of the day or night, whether he was in or not, to go through the sample trays of rocks he kept there, which included even semiprecious stones and geodes that anyone would like to own or could sell. The policy was unusual but he had nothing to hide from his students, and probably no exams sequestered there, and he felt they might need the inspiration from handling a rock of some sort, a sliver of quartz or a chunk of sial. Few were so inspired (at least I never was), but The Rock's little nest was always open, and it was nice to know that we were trusted.

I remembered not to knock, and opened the door about a foot and poked my head in. The Rock sat at his desk, tenderly turning some pieces of dull gray rock, puffing his pipe as if it were an ore smelter. The rocks he handled were most likely just some residue from the earth's mantle, but to him they were clues, and he was Sherlock Holmes in rapture over the find. The little office was as I remembered it from my undergraduate days. There were rocks everywhere, piled to the ceiling, on shelves, in trays. Take one, if you wish. They were his calling cards, pieces of pyrite, orts from the Oligocene, maps to the Mesozoic and beyond. He looked up at me and smiled, over a pair of half-glasses, and bade me to take a seat.

"Good to see you, lad," he said as though I'd just strolled in to take his freshman geology class.

We shook hands and I sat in a small chair in front of his desk. I had not appraised his physical appearance very carefully when I first saw him at Yates Sutherland's party, but it seemed he'd turned much older in the time I'd been away. The years had etched him and, antithetical to the Piedmont, had imposed old age upon his relative youth. Rivulet lines and wrinkles were foliated deep into his face, and he looked a little tired and haggard. His hair looked the same, though, sparse and crew-cut, and I'd always wondered how such a vulnerable dome, a pate so unprotected, could grapple with the universe and master its unimaginably ponderous elements. The Rock had been snidely nicknamed by students who had seen him as a nuisance with a mason's hammer, but I liked to think that he and his science were the foundation of knowledge, the crusty, spunky, sledge-hammer-proof pediment we could depend on. I told him I was glad to see him, and pleased to be a professor now as he was, but I was mindful that my academic discipline was narrow compared with his boundless scope, that the affectations of John Gay and company comprised less than a millionth of a second on his geologic clock.

"Are you still playing tennis, lad?" He tilted his nose up and tried to look at me through the half-glasses, and I hoped he couldn't tell I was disappointed that he seemed to remember only my ability as a jock and not my "genius" in class. He'd been impressed by a point I played years ago, while he stood on the golf course of the Sutherland Country Club waiting to make his shot. The hole overlooked the country club tennis courts, where I happened to be playing at the time, and he saw me play only one point. I happened to win it, in a flurry of reflexive, desperate shots that only a non-tennis player could have mistaken for strategy. "Brilliant!" he called down from his elysian fairway, but I knew better. I had only fumbled to winning, and aeons might pass before I'd again grope to such "genius."

"I play, occasionally," I admitted, then I told him I had come to discuss more important matters. I reached for the rock I had in the pocket of my jacket, and deposited the quartz-like, golf ball-sized lump amid the debris on top of his desk. He squinted at it a moment, through his half-glasses and then over them, and then bent down for an even closer look. He scooped the rock up, cupped it in his hands, and brought it so close to his face that I thought he would eat it.

"Do you know what you have here, lad?"

"No, sir."

"Where did you find it?"

"In a pink T'bird." I chuckled a little, but he saw no joke. After all, he was comfortable with the knowledge that entire continents skated about the globe and that oceans and mountain ranges galloped nomadic. Certainly he could accept the most outrageous clue in stride and easily believe that my rock had materialized from behind the spare tire of Warren The Queer's little pink car.

"You think it's a diamond, lad?" He winked at me and shifted the crystalline golf ball from one hand to the other. "It's probably quartz, you know," he continued. "Heavy, though. Maybe eight or nine hundred carats."

"That's big, isn't it?"

"Bigger than ever found in this country. In fact, not more than a single-carat stone has ever been found here."

"You mean diamonds, not quartz."

"Precisely, lad."

It was foolish to think that it was a diamond, but I felt like more of a fool for not having told the detective about it, as it may have been a motive in Cowpens Martin's murder.

"It's very dull," I said.

"So are some of my students, until they're polished." He took a large magnifying glass from his desk drawer and stared at the cloudy lump. He shifted the focus again and again in the bad light, and I could only think of Sherlock Holmes and the poor, archaic instruments he must have had.

"I'd like to get it under a high-powered microscope in the lab," he continued, "after I remove the coating of ferrous oxide."

"Ferrous oxide? My chemistry's rusty."

"So's the stone, so to speak. From traveling by water. The ferrous oxide indicates an alluvial source. . . ." He gazed through the magnifying glass for a long time, turning the stone very slowly.

Finally he looked up and asked, "Where'd you say you got this, lad?"

I was sure that he was far less interested in the monetary value of the possible gem than in its origin, but I did not give him the note it had come wrapped up in. Apparently in Cowpens Martin's handwriting, a surprisingly clear hand with perfect spelling, the note explained that he had found the stone while working out on roadcut number 42 in Sutherland County. After that, I assumed, he'd simply brought it back to Mrs. Carswell's and tucked it behind the spare tire of Warren's pink T'bird, where I found it. I told The Rock, however, that I'd found it out near a roadcut when I had to stop because my car overheated. He considered the information a moment and then told me it could be a diamond, but not to get my hopes up. If it was, he added intriguingly, it was a whopper.

"But most diamonds come from Africa, don't they?"

"Right, lad. And from India, Russia, Brazil, and Murfreesboro, Arkansas."

"Arkansas?"

"There was an actual diamond mine there, a true kimberlite pipe like the ones in South Africa."

Seeing my quizzical expression, he went on to explain that a kimberlite pipe was a volcanic blowhole that brought diamonds to the surface from molten rock seventy-five miles or so beneath the earth's crust.

"Could there be diamonds in South Carolina?"

"You bet, lad. A fellow over in Spartanburg found one once, and others have been found from time to time along the Blue Ridge Wall. It was puny stuff, though. Poor quality too. Basically worthless."

"And in Sutherland County?"

"The volcanic activity was here."

"And diamonds could have been brought to the surface?" I thought he might call me a genius for filling in the obvious blank, but I'd been tricked.

"There's no kimberlite here." He shook his head. "And no evidence of carbon either. And you know, of course, that diamonds are made from carbon."

"Then what came up in the volcanoes?"

"Good question, lad. The rock here is called 'ultra-sima,' and it does not necessarily bear diamonds. It takes a lot to make one: millions of tons of pressure per square inch and five thousand degrees temperature. And some diamonds, you know, are eight hundred million years old."

I was shocked. Not so much about what it took to make a diamond, but about what wonderful stories he had compared with the ones I had to tell my English classes. I wanted to know more.

"If this were one, would there be others?"

"I've found several here in Sutherland County, but they were too puny to mention," he said modestly, but I detected a certain amount of pride.

Mosquito shit, I thought, but didn't tell him what Carlos's father would have called his find.

"You see, lad, glaciation and erosion have long since leveled the volcanoes that brought diamonds to the earth's surface, and the ones that made it to the top have been moved all over the place. You'd have to look long and hard to find a diamond in the first place, and be damned lucky to find another, let alone one of this unprecedented size." He picked up the stone again and hefted it in the palm of one hand. Then he let it roll off his fingers onto the desk and relit his pipe, which had gone out during our conversation.

I concluded that Cowpens had left just a dull gray stone, no more remarkable than any other from the earth's crust, a clouded quartz mirror of his own crusty, washed-out life. Still, The Rock wanted to keep it and examine it further, and he insisted that I show him where I found it. I agreed to a field trip together, and was excited at the prospect, though I didn't have a clue as to where roadcut 42 was, and had only Cowpens's cryptic note to guide me. Lucky for me, though, The Rock first wanted time to clean up the stone and look at it in the lab. So I left it with him, more on the basis of thinking it was worthless than on implicit trust, and headed to the college library to see if they had a county surveyor's map, and if I could find roadcut 42.

$\triangledown$

Chapter 10

THE SUTHERLAND COLLEGE LIBRARY was a classic structure, as comfortable as an old gymnasium, with wooden floors darkened from years of polish and good, honest sweat. The sweat of my brow was in there, where I'd sequestered myself and pored over my books as an undergraduate, to get away from the noise in the dorms and ever-partying loudmouths like Yates Sutherland.

As I bounded up the steps, I noticed an old black man watering some bushes, who'd been there during my undergraduate days. He smiled and said "Afternoon, sir," as though he recognized me, and as though I'd never left the place. I answered, "Afternoon to you too, sir," and recalled the consternation of my Southern companions when they'd heard me address the old black folk of the campus as "sir" or "ma'am."

I opened the front screen door, and the rusty hinges and return spring produced a racket that seemed to bother an elderly librarian who stood guard just inside at a great oaken desk.

"May I help you, young man?" She seemed indignant that I had entered and upset the balance of things. I liked that she had called me young man, however, and I noticed that she had been reading a book of stories by Eudora Welty, which she set quickly aside as though she knew I was a Yankee and shouldn't see those sacred writings of the South.

"I could use some help, ma'am, if you don't mind my intruding." I used my most polite tone, and even affected a slight Southern drawl, but she saw right through me. She stared and said not a word, and I awkwardly explained that I was looking for some county surveyor's maps but wouldn't have the slightest idea where to find them, or how to look them up in the card catalogs. She remained silent so I introduced myself and explained that I taught English at the college.

"Now, what would an English professor be wantin' with surveyor's maps?" She adjusted her glasses.

"It's a special assignment," I mumbled, which did not convince her but finally got her to rise.

"Follow me." She led me through the library, all the way to the back and down some creaky stairs to the research section in the basement. It was slow going and I asked her if she needed a hand on the stairs, but she shook her head and stated proudly, "Ah'm quite in control."

She was indeed in control, and when I stumbled slightly on a loose stair she was quick to notice and say, "May I assist you, young man?"

In the basement, she led me through a maze of tomes stacked on sagging shelves, and finally brought me to a dust-covered pile of maps in a remote corner. I thanked her and began to look through them. She watched me a moment and then stated, with great authority, "These are not to be removed," before marching off, probably to her guard post upstairs at the front desk.

I found roadcut 42 on one of the first maps I looked at. It jumped out at me, as though it had been written in Cowpens

Martin's own hand. It was located where the Blue Ridge Wall had stopped Interstate 26 from going up to Asheville, at a deep cut in the mountains called Green River Gorge. The highway department had built a magnificent bridge across the gorge, but had never connected the bridge with the interstate. Roadcut 42 was at the south end of the span, where they'd blasted a narrow channel through a rise so they could reach the gorge, but the only access to it was by an unpaved work road through the woods. At least, that's what I surmised from the map, and it was pretty recent.

Satisfied that I could find the roadcut, if I had to take The Rock, I replaced the maps and wandered through the research section until I found some books about diamonds. They were suitably tucked away in the deepest, darkest recesses of that ancient building, and I plucked them out and sat down with them at a small study desk nearby. I skimmed mostly, but occasionally stopped to read the tale of some fabulous gem that a slave or a panhandler had kicked up in the dust somewhere, that had gone through a rapid, bloody change of hands, only to end up as an ornament in the crown of some fat-cat monarch. For the most part, the stories were tragic. The slaves who had found the gems always coughed them up for their masters and always wound up dead or relegated forever to their squalor. Nothing changes, I thought. Poor Cowpens had coughed up his gem, if it were one, and wound up dead, never having bettered his lot. I shivered a little and vowed not to have my life snuffed out for a few lousy carats.

I soon became absorbed in the romance of the musty old volumes around me. The walls of books formed the passageway of a diamond mine and the little reading lamp on the desk was the light on my miner's helmet. I kicked and clawed through the rubble and dust, until I found my prize. And then I rose from the depths, from the dankness and the squalor, and escaped from the Peachblossom Motel and Mrs. Carswell's and the misery I'd felt since my first night in the South. I was Diamond Jim Brady and I went back to New York a hero, where my wife and my sweet child waited with open arms. And I lived with them forever in wealth's self-esteem. . . .

Suddenly I sensed another presence in the diamond mine passageway behind me. It must be the old lady, I thought, coming to tell me not to remove books from the research section. But when I turned to look, I was startled and jumped to my feet. It was none other than Yates Sutherland.

"Easy, boy." Scaring me had amused him.

"You should have warned me." My daydream eroded and my diamond mine passageway collapsed. I was just another wage slave confronted by his master. Nothing changes. Heraclitus was wrong. The world would always oppress with a weight that turned diamonds to dust.

"Good to see my professors so deeply involved in their work." He laughed as though he were at his faculty party, with a glass of Southern Comfort in his fat hand.

"That's not funny," I said.

"Watcha readin', boy?" He ignored my complaint and edged toward my stack of books.

"Nothing special. . . ."

He reached around me and, with the big gold head of his cane, spread the stack apart as though it were a deck of cards. "Diamonds." He squinted. "Didn't know you were teachin' a class on them, boy."

"I'm not, actually. . . ."

He grabbed a book and flipped through the pages. "Looka this whopper." He held a pudgy finger on the color plate of a very large diamond with a blue cast.

"Sonofabitch that found that'd be mighty lucky. What do you think, boy?" He held the picture toward me and cracked the spine of the book and smeared the plate with his oily fingers.

"I'd like to find it."

"Careful, boy. Big diamonds have big, bad curses that go with 'em. Leastwise, that's what I heard."

"I'd take my chances."

As we spoke, he leaned his cane against the desk, drew a pair of reading glasses from his inside coat pocket, and put them on to read the caption under the color plate. "I believe you would take a chance on this one. It's more than a thousand carats." He looked at me over the top of his glasses. "Why, I believe I might take a chance on it myself." His look hardened and he seemed to examine me, as though through a jeweler's loupe.

"Could you hang onto somethin' like this, boy, even if it wasn't rightfully your own?" He set the tortured book down, and I stiffened as I watched him remove and refold his glasses and then smile again as he tucked them back inside his coat.

"Don't be upset, now. It's just an appraisal—of character." He slapped my shoulder. "And I'm talking' strength of character. Why, my own granddaddy took over this whole damn county by gettin' and holdin' onto land that wasn't rightfully his own. And I admire the man."

Before I could comment, he picked up his cane and, without another word, disappeared as quickly and mysteriously as he'd come. I knew he was eccentric, but I had to wonder what he'd meant. The Rock wouldn't have told him anything, or he'd have brought it into the open. I told myself it was nothing but the rambling of a wealthy college president, but I hastily put the books away and left the library.

It was growing dark as I walked to my car. Classes were over for the day, and the campus was nearly empty for the weekend. My crappy Tempest stood alone in the parking lot and I got in, with nowhere to go but back to my rooming house.

On the way, I fantasized about my would-be diamond. It would be a historical find and would deserve a special name. "The Star of Sutherland" came to mind first, and then I cringed at the thought. That was Yates's name too, and I rejected the notion that everything significant from the area should bear his moniker just because he'd been born with a few extra bucks. "The Carolina Moon" might do . . . no, too corny, and real diamonds sparkled more than the moon. . .

"The Jim Harrington" was a thought . . . or, better yet, "The Big Jimbo" . . . No, it was Cowpens Martin's stone after all, and rightly it should be called "The Cowpens." Ugh! The poor little man deserved all the recognition and money it might bring, but that name made it sound as though it had been found under a meadow muffin. Besides, it wouldn't help him now. Anyway, great diamonds should have great names. I knew of only two: The Hope Diamond and Yankee Stadium. When I thought of the black history of the former and of George Steinbrenner's troubles with the latter, I hoped I would never be so cursed. Still, I cursed myself for not telling the detective about it, and wondered why I wanted anything at all to do with the rock from the Sutherland County roadcut.

$\triangledown$

Chapter 11

I SEEMED TO FIT in at Mrs. Carswell's now. My Tempest
no longer announced its arrival with the squeaking song of
the humpback whale. I'd had the water pump fixed. And the
driver's side door no longer violated the fastidious surround-
ings with its creaking groan. I'd had the hinges greased. I
had Yates Sutherland to thank for that, and the advance he'd
given me to coach the tennis team. I felt guilty that I had
not scheduled any fall practices. The days were still warm,
but Cowpens's murder seemed to have killed the summer.
Almost overnight the leaves had turned and rained on
Magnolia Street, and buried the lawns of the Southern
Simple houses. The nights were crisp and the days percep-
tibly shorter. Going to bed and then waking up in my room
had been eerie; for days I'd been alone. I hadn't seen Warren,
and I never saw Mrs. Carswell, and Cowpens's empty room
with its door partly open echoed the forlorn spirit of the
pathetic little man. I missed him and his turnip-green
twang, and strangely sage comments on life. He was an
educated man, and we would have been friends.

Upstairs at Mrs. Carswell's, I was surprised to find Warren seated at the kitchen table with a half-empty whiskey
bottle in front of him. His eyes were red, the lids swollen,

and he looked more exhausted than drunk. I told him I was sorry about Cowpens and he answered by telling me he'd been picked up by the police and held all week in jail for questioning. They'd been rough on him.

At first I felt guilty that he, Cowpens's dearest friend, had had to bear the brunt of the investigation while I, a virtual stranger, had waltzed away. On the basis of that thinking, however, it seemed odd that Cowpens had turned the stone over to me and had never mentioned it to Warren. Or had he? I was no longer sure that Warren was completely harmless, for who knows what greed can do. It was mere curiosity, not greed, I told myself that had made me withhold evidence in the murder.

Suddenly I stopped feeling sorry for Warren, and began worrying about sleeping there if he was going to be around. Perhaps it was not too late to turn the stone over to the police. I could tell them I'd stumbled on it while looking at the pink T'bird. No, that was Warren's car and it would really put him in the soup, and he might kill me in my sleep just for that. . . .

"He was such a sweet man," Warren said quite soberly, then took a very small sip from the whiskey bottle, grimaced, and put it down. "I don't mean sweet like people might think," he continued, "as he never shared my preferences, you know."

I knew only that I did not fully trust him anymore. But I decided to suffer him a little longer, if only for Cowpens's sake, or the reason that, seated before me with his hands so primly placed now upon his knees, looking like a frail little old lady at tea, he seemed so pathetic.

"I hope you don't mind," he said. "I have to talk to someone. He was my only true friend, and he was so very gentle. . . ."

"Who could have hurt him?"

" ... and he was kind and considerate ... " he went on as though he hadn't heard my question.

"He had nothing worth stealing?" I tried warily. This time he stopped and looked at me, and thought a moment before he answered.

"He only had his job. He drank his puny salary, and sometimes I helped him to pay his rent."

"Who else did he know?"

"Now you sound like a detective." He smiled crookedly, and abruptly rose from the chair. The sudden shift in mood was odd. I hadn't wished to offend him. I had only wanted to know more, and I told him so. Still, he ignored me and made for the door.

"Who else did he know?" I asked again.

He stopped and faced me, as though he might answer, but nothing came out. I shall never forget that last vacant look in his eyes as he walked out, shutting the door behind him.

I went to my room, thinking again about the stone. I wanted it to be a diamond, and I wanted it. That's all it came down to. I deserved some recompense for my pain, for the low point to which my life had sunk. I looked for some allegory in the overworked good-versus-evil motif, and pondered some more whether to tell or not to tell the cops. But I wrestled only briefly with my conscience, and managed to convince myself that it was all just an exercise until I found out whether I owned an outrageously big diamond or only a godforsaken worthless little chunk of the Carolina countryside. The Rock hadn't gotten back to me for almost a week, so I wasn't encouraged.

Before lying down and closing my eyes, I made sure the door was securely locked, and wedged a chair under the doorknob.

$\bigtriangledown$

Chapter 12

 T HE NEXT MORNING, SATURDAY, I woke to the sound of pouring rain. I'd loved mornings like it when I was in college, when I could lie warm and tucked in bed until the spirit moved me to rise at noon or so for lunch. I could sleep then. I was innocent. I had only to hide from homework and classes, and Sutherland College was a grand hotel on the Isle of Tranquility that, with a few more luxuries could have been the Greenbrier. Now I only worked there as one of the luxuries, the servant who brought the kids Beowulf after breakfast and mollycoddled them through Middle English as though I were a genteel old white-coated waiter coming around with a second cup of coffee. That morning, the cold November rain forced me out of bed and sent me shivering across Mrs. Carswell's icy linoleum floor to shut the window. Thus I was up for the day, a full-fledged workingman, inured to life's hardships, steeled to the fact that the sheets I'd bought at Sears were not as warm as the ones my old man had paid for from the college linen service.

In Saratoga Springs, such a rain at this time of year would have been a snowstorm. My little daughter would have wakened me with chirps and squeals and warmth and drool. The old Victorian house we rented would have warmed us when the rattling pipes clanked their steam up to the hissing radiators. My wife would have made me breakfast, and the coffee would have been real, not the powdered stuff I'd been stirring all these days at Mrs. Carswell's stark kitchen. My daughter, my sweetest of little girls, would giggle in her gruel and whip her spoon in the air to form arcs of oatmeal on the kitchen wallpaper. Then, meal finished or not, she'd punctuate the effort by spiking her cereal bowl to the floor. I'd cursed the mess but I loved it, and I'd have paid dearly on that gray November day to have it back. Work would be the antidote to such feelings, I thought as I showered and dressed. I'd do my job and pour my being into it, and the rotten day would dissolve.

I toted my briefcase into Mrs. Carswell's kitchen and began to grade papers while I had breakfast. My freshman English students had written an essay, a purely creative piece on the subject of their choice in any length and form. The only criterion I'd set for them was that the paper had to be submitted on a certain date. While I waited for water to boil on Mrs. Carswell's old gas stove, I shuffled through their submissions and the first essay that caught my eye was titled, "The Humorous Complexities of the Social Life of the American College Student," by Joan Funk. Just from the title, I wanted to flunk Miss Funk, but I wanted even less to wade through her twenty-seven single-spaced pages. So I shuffled on to another paper, by one of the football players. It was untitled and read, in its entirety:

I love to hit and block. I love to clothesline guys when they come through the line. It's good when their necks snap and they get whiplash. They must get a headache that feels like an ice pick in their brain. When I am out with the team, I love to drive my elbow through plaster-and-sheetrock barroom walls. I test the wall first now, since I hit a stud once and broke it (my arm). I hope I get an "A" on this paper because I flunked every test.

I gave him an *A*. He'd written about something he loved, said it clearly and well, and hadn't made me wade through twenty-seven pages. I shuffled some more, trying to find another catchy theme that could brighten a bleak November morning and make my instant coffee taste a little better. Loquita Scruggs's paper surprised me. For some reason, I'd expected her to write some pullaver about the glorious old antebellum South, or something as innocuous, but she regaled me with a shocking and erotic account of her trip to New York City as a high-school senior. Titled "Punk," her paper described her experience in terms of bars and rock concerts, and she ended with a graphic description of a girl orally servicing men for a buck a throw in the restroom at a Van Halen concert. By the time the cops got to the girl, Miss Scruggs wrote, she'd collected more than fifty dollars.

I gave Miss Scruggs an *A*. She had a strong journalistic style, perhaps a little too much like the *National Enquirer*, and she wasn't afraid to say anything. Then I decided to give everybody an *A* just for turning in a paper. I realized it wasn't fair to penalize Miss Funk for her dry, lengthy composition and reward Miss Scruggs for her pithy, wet one. Besides, the students' papers would carry little or no weight toward their overall grades. This was merely an exercise that would give me an idea of their likes and dislikes, of their strengths and weaknesses, and of how much work each of them was willing to put into a project with so few parameters. Of course I would read them all quite thoroughly, even Miss Funk's twenty-seven pager, but I decided that one would have to wait when I discovered Bonnie Weber's paper. I had not expected it. She had been excused from classes for the week by a note from Mrs. Sutherland, explaining that she'd be in Charleston preparing for a concert. I didn't mind. She'd easily make it up, and what was freshman English compared to singing with the Charleston Symphony. Her paper had a provocative title, and I expected more lewd behavior at a Van Halen concert or, more likely for Bonnie, at a Bach concert. I was not disappointed, however, that it turned out to be a pretty good Medieval morality tale, which was obviously a message for me. And though it made me feel somewhat shabby, I include it here as evidence of my selfish character from another point of view.

The Tale of the Creepy Choirmaster
and the Salacious Soprano
by Bonnie Weber

The pure resonance of the castrati rang through the groined vaults of the ancient cathedral where Grundig the Choirmaster held practice. Grundig grinned as the sound swelled higher, transported on the fears and sweat of the tiny, trembling sparrows in the pews below. For if one of them faltered or erred, he'd surely hear it and turn his gaze from the heavens down upon the offender, and banish the errant voice from the cathedral forever, to the plague, pestilence, fire, and damnation that waited for all outside.

It was during the Nunc Dimittis that Grundig first noticed the pale, almost pretty soprano, Esmerelda, the only one who dared to return his stare, with a slight, strange smile. He was unnerved to be so challenged, though he did not show it, and her voice was perfect, so he moved on to the one that was ever so slightly off pitch. His fat face reddened as he pointed his index fingers like the horns of the devil, and shouted, "Be gone!"

The poor child heaved and sobbed and shuffled his way out forever. All eyes were averted, of course, except those of Esmerelda, and her slight, strange smile of adoration, despite the wicked expulsion, had not changed.

Was it divine rapture, he wondered, or was she possessed by demons? Had her voice not been so perfect and her pale, almost pretty visage so intriguing, he would have declared her possessed and expelled her, or worse.

But he moved on, and made them perform the most difficult of canticles, and their sound was never so full or so fine. He grinned and rolled his eyes to Heaven, but the smile and the voice of the pale Esmerelda played on his mind. Soon he could hear only her crystal-clear soprano, through the glissandi and cadenzas, as it haunted and tantalized. And always, when he dared to look, she smiled her strange smile.

Soon he feared that she was the succubus, and that his preoccupation verged on lechery, one of the deadliest sins. And so one day, after choir practice was over, after she'd loosed the last rapturous note, he called her to his living chamber behind the apse. He lurked inside his chamber by a flickering candle, like some gargoyle, with a crucifix behind him on the wall. "I've noticed you," he said as he motioned her to enter, "and your voice is to be complimented, indeed." Her smile widened but his voice turned to ice as he continued, "But you distract the choir, so they envy you, one of the deadliest sins."

"Dismiss them, Choirmaster," she said boldly. "The envy is their sin, not mine."

His face reddened and he rose from his chair. "Pride," he hissed, "will not help your plight." She dropped to her knees and kissed the grubby, frayed hem of his robe, and through desperate sobs told him she would do anything not to be expelled. Her cheek against his thigh was more than he could stand. "You are purged of your sins, my child." He shuddered. "And you are free of this holy place. Be gone" He pushed her away.

The next day, and for the rest of his life, Grundig the Choirmaster lorded over the little voices of the cathedral, but nevermore was he transported by them, and evermore did he search in vain for the pure, rapturous voice of the banished Esmerelda.

Okay, I was Grundig, The Creepy Choirmaster who would more likely than not banish true beauty from my life. Bonnie, The Salacious Soprano, had admired me and tried to please me the only way she knew how. But it bothered me to be perceived as one more devoted to academic discipline than to the pursuit of beauty and truth. I had allowed that everpresent student-teacher thing—that harmless flirtation that occurs from kindergarten through graduate school, in all disciplines, in which the teacher seduces certain of his or her progeny into learning, and is in turn seduced by them. Figuratively, of course. Bonnie must have taken my lecture

on the carpe diem philosophy in poetry too much to heart:
perhaps I shouldn't have flirted with her on that one. She
was too strong-willed and too inclined to seize the day, if she
could. I, on the other hand, was too much like Milton's Il
Penseroso, the pensive man who would deny the vain,
deluding joys. What could I do without banishing her forever
to unemotional note-taking? As the day went on and I graded
more papers, I felt more and more like the miserable old
Grundig in his chamber, cloistered at Mrs. Carswell's from
the November chill. I finally fell asleep reading Joan Funk's
twenty-seven pager.

I awoke at six in the evening. It was dark outside and the
rain had stopped. As I lay on my bed and stared at the
ceiling, for a few precious moments my mind was free from
the clutter of all the papers I'd corrected, and from my worry
and guilt about the mess of my life. Then I remembered the
note that Carlos had left for me with the college reception-
ist. He wanted me to come by his jewelry shop that Saturday
evening before he closed at seven. Only if I felt like it, he
wrote, to go have a few drinks and take in the Sutherland
nightlife as we used to. I had pushed it to the back of my
mind, feeling that we could not avoid the subject of Jody.
Since he'd asked her to marry him, and she hadn't given an
answer, he'd certainly want to know if I had anything to do
with her hesitation. He'd want to know my intentions,
though I had none, particularly after the disastrous night
at Elmer's Tradewinds. I felt she'd never want to see me
again.

I should stay away from Carlos, I thought, since his fierce
pride and terrible temper could create an ugly scene. But I
was bored from long days in the classroom and from long
evenings at Mrs. Carswell's, and I was just plain curious

about what he might have to say. So I jumped out of bed, pulled on some clothes, and made it to his shop a few minutes before seven.

$\triangledown$

Chapter 13

THE GARCIA'S SHOP ALWAYS looked closed. It was some-thing in the facade, the way that Carlos and his father had tastefully sealed over the front windows and inserted small shadow-box displays here and there, each highlighting a single piece of their custom-designed jewelry. The look was unique in Sutherland, where broken-down pawnshops and old junk jewelry stores with their brummagem wares fes-tooned under bright fluorescent lights across big plate-glass windows looked as if they were open twenty-four hours of the day. And as though a shopper might need more infor-mation on what was inside, there was always a big, lighted plastic sign, faded and cracked, with letters and lightbulbs missing, that gave the name of the store and the latest bargains. The only sign on the Garcia's was a small bronze plaque beside the entrance that read *Garcia and Son, Fine Jewelry*. The effect was quite elegant, ala Tiffany's in New York, but as I approached I was afraid that Carlos had already closed and I stopped and looked into one of the dark, velvet-lined display cases before trying the door. There on an ivory pedestal, enhanced by a hidden spotlight, was a gold ring of the most intricate design, with a huge, exquisite stone the most delicate shade of blue. The display was more dramatic than that of the Hope Diamond at the Smithsonian. I pressed my nose to the window for a closer look and found that I could see, as through a tunnel, into the shop.

There, to my surprise, were Carlos and Yates Sutherland. They did not see me, and I watched a moment as Yates grimly thudded a fat fist on one of the glass counters and poked at Carlos with his gold-headed cane. Carlos gestured wildly and chattered a mile a minute, as though in rapid Portuguese. The glass I looked through was thick, and I could not hear a word.

I moved quickly away and waited outside a few minutes. They were probably arguing about the diamond brooch Carlos was making for Yates, and it would be an awkward time to enter, so I looked around the mall. It had been a remarkable renovation since my student days when Sutherland was virtually a one-stoplight burg and when a dilapidated movie theater and six filthy pool halls were the main attractions. Since then, Main Street had been closed to automobiles and paved over with brick in a smart herringbone pattern. The rusted old cast-iron streetlights and stanchions had been replaced with exotic poles of spun aluminum and fancy square lamps of a pseudogaslight treatment. There were also a good-sized foundation and several comfortable seating areas surrounded with carefully shaped hedges and delicate little trees. It suddenly occurred to me that I was the only person standing out there on the mall, since most of the stores had already been closed and it looked like more rain. Then a few drops hit me and I thought I'd better get into the shop whether Carlos and Yates had finished arguing or not. As I opened the door, Yates stopped in midsentence with his mouth open and his index finger pointed at Carlos.

"Is this a stickup?" I asked, since Yates's finger looked like a gun.

"That's a good one, boy." He turned his finger-gun toward me and ceremoniously shook my hand. "But he's the one does the stickin' up." He nodded at Carlos, who shifted nervously and tried to laugh.

I went along with Yates's little joke and made a great show of inspecting the shop's interior. Everywhere I looked I nodded in approval of the elegant but always tasteful decor. Carlos was proud and Yates was amused. I thought it was too bad he hadn't brought his wife in for a lesson in interior decorating from the Garcias.

"Ain't bad for a wetback." Yates tried to carry the joke a little further, but Carlos failed to smile, and I cringed. In our friendship over the years, Carlos and I had called each other a lot of names in fun, but "wetback" was one I would never have dared to use.

I quickly tried to change the subject. "I'm only interested in one thing."

"What's that, boy?" Yates chimed in as though he owned the shop, and Carlos remained silent.

"The big diamond in the front window."

"Diamond?" Carlos finally spoke.

"The one with the blue cast, in the black velvet showcase."

"Hah! He wishes that was a diamond." Yates slapped me on the back. "It's some crap they mine by the ton in Brazil, boy, and it ain't worth the settin' it's settin' in."

"It's a tourmaline," Carlos said stiffly, more to Yates than to me. "And it happens to be a very good one."

"Oh, 'prima qualita,'" I used one of Carlos's favorite Portuguese expressions, and he laughed and relaxed a little, finally paying more attention to me than to Yates.

"Ain't nothin' second-rate in this boy's store." Yates sensed he'd been left out and tried a compliment to get back in our favor. But it was too late, and the three of us stood a moment in awkward silence trying to think of something more to say. Finally, Yates spoke again and told us he had to leave.

He threw a glance at Carlos as he reached for the front door. "We'll talk Monday." Carlos shrugged and said nothing, and Yates opened the door and disappeared into the night.

"I didn't mean to interrupt a business transaction," I said as Carlos began to unlock the sliding doors behind the glass display counters in the showroom and pull the trays of jewelry out and set them on top.

"No big deal." A diamond bracelet slipped off one of the trays and fell to the floor. Carlos swore in Portuguese as he stooped to pick it up and then disdainfully flipped it back up onto the tray as though it were a piece of food that was no good once it had become dirty. Whether it was a show for me or not, I knew his father would have objected to such rough treatment of the merchandise. I wondered if he was the kind who would treat a woman roughly once he was used to her and her value had diminished in his eyes.

"It's a big deal to me," I said, "if you and Yates were talking about the brooch you're making for his wife, the one with all the diamonds."

"That was finished weeks ago, man."

When the trays he wanted out were all on top of the glass cases, he went around and stacked them one on top of another, as a busboy might stack cafeteria trays. He told me they had to go into the safe and, picking up a pile of them, slipped out of the showroom into a back office.

"You put everything away?" I called out.

"Only the precious stones. The shit we leave out for the thieves." He returned quickly with a big grin on his face and, with a little samba dance, picked up the remaining pile of

trays and took them into the back. I felt that, in spite of his
attempts to appear cool and casual, he knew precisely where
everything was, right down to the tiniest tourmaline. I
thought about testing him, just slipping some little carbun-
cle into my pocket to see if he'd notice. I decided against it,
however, since he might not consider it funny, and it might
kill any vestige of trust that was left between us since my
interest in Jody had become apparent. Suddenly, he re-
emerged and brushed by me to unlock the showcases in the
front window.

"These have to be put away too." He carefully removed
the ring I'd noticed when I was standing outside on the mall.

"But you said it was a semiprecious stone, shit to leave
out for the thieves."

"True, but the rednecks would think it was a diamond
and smash the window." He cleared out the other showcases
and disappeared again into the back, where he stayed for a
few moments, probably putting the stuff into the safe. I
thought about his comment that the rednecks would think
the semiprecious stone was a diamond. If he laughed at
them, he'd surely laugh at me for all I'd gone through, for
thinking that a dirty old hunk of quartz was a diamond and
for withholding it from the police when I knew very well it
could be evidence in a murder investigation. With such lack
of intelligence and foresight, I was no better than any dumb
redneck who would smash a jewelry shop window for a cheap
tourmaline, and no less guilty than the redneck who bashed
in Cowpens Martin's head.

But was it a redneck who did Cowpens in behind Elmer's?
Carlos's statement had made me think. A redneck would
want something sharp-looking and shiny since, like Shakespeare's fools, he'd believe it had to glitter to be gold. He might
smash a window for a tawdry tourmaline, as Carlos said, but

he was unlikely to bash in a skull for a dull, uncut stone. No, if Cowpens was killed for the stone, it was someone who knew all about diamonds in the rough and otherwise, not a dumb redneck. I followed what I thought was a logical progression, and felt much like a smart detective, until I ran into the stone wall of fact: it wasn't a diamond. At least I thought it wasn't since The Rock hadn't contacted me in a week. He'd had plenty of time to examine it. Probably he'd found it to be mere quartz and tossed it off into one of the dusty trays of rocks in his office, forgetting to call me.

I was relieved to think that the stone was nothing. It eased my guilt and my worry that someone sinister might be laying for me out on the damp, chilly mall. Someone who might think I'd taken the stone to a jeweler for appraisal and would go back to Mrs. Carswell's, where he'd skulk in Cowpens's empty room, and wait for me to return so he could bash my head in and take the diamond. But, thank goodness, it wasn't a diamond, and Cowpens had probably been wasted in a back-alley squabble over who would buy the beer. It was either that or a confrontation with a foolish, desperate mugger who thought the wretched little man might have some pocket money worth taking, and who got all that Cowpens had, his toughness and his pride when he faced up to him. In either case, turning the stone over to the police now would do nothing to bring him back and nothing to solve his murder. It would only put me in jail for withholding evidence or for suspicion of murder. So I decided that the stone would simply have to lie for another billion years, to molder in a sample tray in The Rock's office, to crumble into dust along with Cowpens and me and everybody else, in homage to the vastness of geologic time. . . .

"Wake up, man." Carlos startled me from my daydream. "I hope you were thinking about chicks," he said. "Where we're going, you have to fight them off." He turned off the showroom lights and danced his little Samba toward the door. I followed.

We took separate cars, Carlos in his shiny new Mercedes and me behind in my faded, ancient Tempest. He suggested we take two cars so one of us could leave if he scored and the other didn't. I agreed, but not for that motive. I just wanted my car in case we got into an argument about Jody.

Chapter 14

THE EL CID RESTAURANT, bar, and gathering place took up the entire basement of a large new office building on the outskirts of town. Carlos and I parked at the rear of the building, where the entrance to El Cid was, and walked together down a long, wide flight of stairs to a subterranean maze of dining tables hidden in dark cul de sacs and deep Moorish archways. Simulated torches dimly lit the walls, making it difficult to tell whether the waiters and waitresses were serving or just so many zombies skulking about in that catacomb. And the blocky, metal-studded Castilian furniture only added to the low, ponderous effect, until one suddenly came upon "The Grotto." Then everything opened up, and the effect was dramatic. The ceiling was high and the floor dropped low, several steps down that would be difficult navigation for anyone who'd had too much to drink. The torch lights were much brighter in the cavernous Grotto, and there was plenty of action around a massive, lustrously polished wooden and brass bar. Though it was only eight-thirty when Carlos and I arrived, the place was "packed with chicks" as he had promised. I was not worried that I would have to fight them off, though. I'd always had to work harder than most to meet girls, and the real concern for me at El Cid was how I'd get out of there if a fire started.

We stepped down into The Grotto and nudged our way through the crowd to the bar. Carlos grinned like an idiot and did his little samba while he ogled every girl in the room. He was in his element, to be sure, but to me he was a ridiculous jack-in-the-box who constantly bobbed up and down to view any "chick" behind anyone taller than he.

He elbowed me. "Check those two. Whaddya say we move in on them."

Within the moment it took me to realize who he was talking about, two other guys had approached the girls and struck up a conversation.

"Piranhas!" he spat in disgust. "You have to be quick in here or they get the chicks before you do."

We bought drinks and circled the room. Carlos was a piranha, but I was more like a minnow. I had never enjoyed the bar scene: the initial fluttery come-on, the inane exchange of names, the lies about professions, and the vain hashing-out of aspirations. It was all too forced for me and too desperate. I had separated the males' approach into two categories: The Hollywood Star, and the Comedian. I was not sure where I fit, but Carlos was certainly the Comedian with his little dance, his flip remarks, and blatant sexuality. What was funniest of all, and perhaps most pathetic, was that he thought himself a smooth charmer, the Hollywood Star. His accent helped him though. It gave a woman the chance to ask where he was from, and him the chance to launch into his patented discourse on Brazil and the exotic nature of Rio, which he represented as his town, as though he weren't stuck like everyone else in the jerkwater burg of Sutherland, South Carolina.

It could be harmless fun, and I don't mean to come across as a complete cynic. I could certainly understand the fantasy of the moment, but it's just that I was a poor practitioner, or perhaps I understood the woman's role all too well. I put that into two categories: "Okay, let's chat," or "Get lost, asshole." I wondered if I'd been too often told to get lost or if I was drawn only to the surly, brooding type of woman who, for some reason I could never fathom, came to jam-packed barrooms to be alone. Each time I was shot down, I was almost sure I hadn't acted like an asshole. I hadn't said anything asinine. I'd been straightforward, unpretentious, mildly amusing, and certainly not The Hollywood Star. I could never be The Comedian and pull a stunt like a guy I'd once seen with a fake telephone concealed under his jacket. He'd make it ring, hand his target the receiver, and say, "It's for you, dear." It was too contrived and too—if you'll excuse the pun—phony. Thus, the whole bar scene seemed phony to me, and I was a mere minnow circling with Carlos and the other piranhas at El Cid that night, watching the would-be Valentinos and the vamps, disdainful of the whole charade but somehow pumped up with the hope of making a score.

"Look at those two, man." Carlos elbowed me. "I bet they speak on the hairy microphone."

"How can you tell?"

He looked at me and grinned and did a frenzied little Samba, spilling part of his drink on the floor.

"Then let's move in before the piranhas." I tried to sound like one of the pack.

He surprised me then, saying, "There are better fish in the sea," and completely ignored the two while he scanned the room for more bait. I, however, kept my eye on the two he'd mentioned and saw that, in the space of a few minutes, they were assailed by several predators, singly and in pairs, who were instantly and callously rebuffed. My type of women, I thought, then realized they must have done the same to

Carlos. I was about to tease him by insisting we go and give them a try, but he suddenly elbowed me again.

"Oooooh, look at that one!" He samba'd furiously in place and nearly drooled over the very attractive young woman who had just entered and found a seat by herself at the bar.

"Go get her," I said.

"You don't mind?" He was shocked to think that a fellow piranha could have some table manners.

"I'll find somebody and join you." My words could be considered a beau geste: the self-sacrifice of the wounded one. They did it all the time in the old westerns, when the hero's partner takes an arrow in the back and, rather than slow the hero down to be overrun by a thousand screaming savages, the partner bravely tells him to go on without him. But my motives were not so noble. First, I wanted to be out of the chase. The competition was too keen for me, a mild-mannered English professor who'd rather sit and take notes, and take what comes along. Second, and most important, I wanted to see the arrogant Carlos, the two-faced lounge-lizard in perpetual heat, who had just asked my old flame to marry him, shot down.

"By the way,"—I held his arm—"come back when she tells you to get lost."

He smirked. "Don't worry about me. Before the night's over, I'll be fucking her between the tits and shooting her in the throat." He made a few thrusting motions with his hips and samba'd away though the crowd. As I watched him go I couldn't imagine how we'd ever double-dated, and how I'd once confided in him about Jody. I remembered telling him about her sweetness and how she'd keep me awake all night and ask for more. He'd countered with tales of some teachers from France he knew who were staying in Sutherland on an exchange program, and who were horny from being so far away from their boyfriends. But where I'd glossed over and kept it pretty much romantic, he told the intimate details, particularly of one who was a Claudine Longet look-alike, who loved to "take it in the ass." I couldn't hate him for those confidences and the laughs we'd shared, but I did wonder why he'd asked Jody to marry him and if he could honor such a contract.

I could see him with the girl at the bar, and hoped I could read her lips when she told him, "Get lost, asshole." To my chagrin, however, they seemed to be involved in a serious discussion and, from my vantage point, she seemed interested in him. I decided to ignore them and bought another drink, thinking it might help me gain his kind of chutzpah or let me more effectively lament the lack of justice in the world. But to my surprise, as I turned from the bar with a fresh drink in hand, I found Carlos standing beside me.

"I need one too." He took my place at the bar and waited to order while I stood quietly by and wondered what had happened. He turned to me and hissed, "Stinking bitch," just as the bartender approached.

"Don't know that one, sir," the bartender said, "but I can make you a Salty Dog or a Fuzzy Navel."

"No, no." Carlos told him what he wanted and then turned back to me. "These bitches are all alike."

"Then you're not going to fuck her between the tits and shoot her in the throat?" I held back a smile and silently applauded the justice in the world, however intermittent it might be.

The bartender brought him his drink and he stirred it and stared at me. Then he gulped half of it down, chuckled, and said earnestly, "You could give her a try."

"If you failed, what chance have I got?"

"She's your type, man."

"Bitchy and frigid?"

"She's an intellectual." He swallowed the remainder of his drink. "She needs a professor."

He seemed sincere, but in case he was not I countered, "You mean she wouldn't prefer a wealthy diamond merchant who could put rings on her fingers and a ruby in her navel?"

"Come on, man. . . ."

"All I can give her is stale poetry."

"That's it. That's what she wants." He turned back to the bar and waited to order another drink.

For a moment I imagined he meant Jody, that he was confessing that she loved me and my stale poetry, not him, and that I should have her. I would have welcomed that beau geste and loved him again, but I realized he did not possess such a noble spirit. I knew that if he loved her, his passion and his fierce pride would never let her go to someone else, especially to someone he knew. If he did love her, though, why was he chasing every girl in the bar? Perhaps his wanting me to try for the girl he'd just failed with was a clue. In the old days, he was much more defensive about being shot down, and always reluctant for me to try in his wake lest I should succeed. It seemed he was urging me to find someone. In fact, the entire evening could have been a setup, an attempt to get me into bed with one of the girls at El Cid so I'd forget about Jody, or so he could report my fickle behavior to her.

All that was pretty farfetched, but I had a vivid imagination, at least vivid enough to believe that an old dull stone from an old dead redneck was akin to the Hope Diamond. Besides, I'd eaten little that day and the alcohol had made me tipsy. As the bartender handed Carlos another drink, I concluded that my imagination was running wild and that I would keep my head and avoid the subject of Jody. I knew his temper, and the drinks he'd had would not allow a rational discussion in that area anyway, so I focused on the girl at the bar.

"My poetry's too bad to try on such a beauty," I told him.

"Go on. . . ."

"No." I shook my head. "Diamonds are probably her best friends and all I've got is a big old rock."

"Rock?" He looked quizzically at me. "Oh, you mean in your pants, man. A big old hard-on."

"I don't mean that." I laughed, "Though I get one on occasion.

"What do you mean?" His eyes narrowed.

I don't know whether the liquor had loosened my tongue, or whether I desired to repair a portion of our strained friendship by letting him in on my secret, but I began to tell him of the stone Cowpens Martin had turned over to me.

"I mean I found a rock. I thought it might be a diamond. Ridiculous, huh?"

Suddenly, he stopped sipping his drink and spoke with the same phony charm he used to pick up girls. And just as suddenly, I became defensive, as any girl might when approached in such a sleazy, oily manner.

"Where did you find this rock?" he asked.

"Just found it." I shrugged. "Don't remember where."

"You don't remember. . . ." His eyes widened.

"I said it's just a rock."

"Sure, sure. Take it easy, man. But you should show it to me. Let me assay it."

"I didn't know you did that."

"Of course." At first he was indignant, but he quickly caught himself and returned to his oily manner. "I went to gemological school. Night classes. I got a degree, man."

"But it's just a rock."

"They've found diamonds in the South."

"Not this big. Almost a thousand carats."

"Carats? Who told you carats?"

"The geology professor over at the college."

"What do geology professors know about diamonds," he scoffed.

"He took some courses too." I was annoyed that he would demean The Rock's vast knowledge on the basis of a few stupid night courses and, with his insistent questions, I was beginning to regret that I'd brought the matter up.

"Okay, man, so he knows diamonds. What did this geology professor, say?"

"He didn't. But he's had the stone a week now and I'm sure he'd have told me if it were valuable."

"You left it with him?"

I nodded, sipped my drink, and looked off into the room for some more attractive girls so we could change the subject, but he continued to stare at me.

"You're very trusting," he said. "People have killed for diamonds, you know."

"Nobody I know."

"What?" He did not understand my play on words."

"I mean I trust him," I said.

"And you say he still has it?"

"He probably threw it out, unless it had some interesting geology. And why are you so interested anyway?"

"Take it easy, man. I'm in the business, and I'm your friend. If you found a thousand-carat diamond, you'd be rich. Famous too. You'd have all these chicks crawling all over you."

"I said it was just a rock."

"So you did," he said slyly, and then neither of us spoke. The silence was as awkward as it had been in his shop with Yates Sutherland earlier that evening. I had only told him

about the rock as a sort of peace offering, a little confidence
that was a joke on myself. I thought he'd laugh and forget,
at least for a moment, that I had undermined his plans with
Jody. I had expected him to blow up about her eventually,
but I had never expected his fusillade of questions about the
rock and that it, not Jody, would heighten the animosity
between us. It was as though he already knew something
about it and thought, as he did about Jody, that it belonged
to him. The silence ticked on, and our years of friendship
seemed to vanish in seconds. The memories of the fun we'd
had together seemed to be gone, the times when nothing was
at stake, when chasing tennis balls and girls meant the same
thing, when we won some and we lost some and no one really
kept score. I knew we'd never recover those days, and it was
only a reflex when I tried once more to set us again on the
case.

"Look at those two," I said. "Whaddya say we talk to
them."

"Huh?" He stared blankly ahead.

"Girls! Are you forgetting what we're here for?"

"They're dogs," he replied without looking at them, "and
this place is a loser."

"But you said it was. . . ."

"Not tonight, man." He set his empty glass on the bar
and turned to leave, but stopped and nodded toward the girl
at the bar he'd tried to pick up. "Stale poetry, that's what
she likes." He smirked and moved his hands, piston-like, in
a halfhearted little samba. Then he left. I bought another
drink, and then another, and watched someone else pick up
the girl at the bar.

I left El Cid at eleven and drove back to Mrs. Carswell's.
The rain had stopped and a full moon had risen, drawing

the heavy clouds with it up into the jet stream high over the Piedmont, where the clouds were thinned and pulled apart into harmless gray mare's tails. The sky was suddenly crisp and cold and far away. A few stars pulsed from between the sections of clouds, signals from another, brighter universe. I felt small and alone. I killed my Tempest in front of Mrs. Carswell's and sat a moment. Magnolia Street was dead. There were no other cars, no people out, and only a few dim lights on in the houses. The trees had died too. Once billowing and lush, they'd turned into hard black outlines, sinister skeletons that rattled in the November nightbreeze.

Odd shapes lurked among the trees and between the houses, and I felt that Cowpens Martin's slayer was stalking me. I shuddered and gooseflesh formed on my arms and crept up and across my chest. Was it fear? Or a sudden chill? I rubbed myself to try to get warm and climbed out of the car. For some reason, I did not hurry inside but stood out on the cold, damp pavement for what seemed an eternity. I had never felt so insignificant, so small and vulnerable. I felt as though I were only a heartbeat away from being flicked off that little curve of the planet into oblivion. And in that precarious, self-demeaned state, my thoughts turned to what I knew best, to my teaching and what I'd recently told my students about the existentialist poets and their celebration of the freedom and uniqueness of man. I'd lied to them. It was that simple. I'd led them to believe that man was free and unique, when I knew that I wasn't, that I was afraid of life and afraid of death and of what might lurk in the shadows on Magnolia Street.

I spurred myself on, wary of the deepest, most threatening shadows, the ones that could hide a man with a club or a knife, and walked around to the side of Mrs. Carswell's house. There, at the entrance to the rooms upstairs, I stopped and looked into her backyard. In the moonlight it appeared clearer than it ever had in the day. The big old barn, the garage, and two other small structures, probably a toolshed and an outhouse, were well-defined in that light and I saw details I'd never noticed. I noticed, too, that something big, something that was always there, was missing—Warren's pink T'bird. It had been a permanent fixture next to the old bar since I'd arrived and I didn't think it ran. But there were only tall grass and weeds in an odd pattern where it had been parked for so long, and I thought he'd either sold it or finally found the old lover he'd bought it for and gone out to run him over, as Cowpens had once told me he would.

As I turned to go upstairs, I looked up at the window of my second-floor room and saw that the light was on. I had left it off. My heart raced and my mind clicked off the possibilities. The maid? No. She never cleaned on Saturdays when the tenants were likely to be home. Warren? Maybe. But I had locked the door and even if he'd gotten in somehow, he was the fastidious type who'd certainly have turned the light off when he left. Mrs. Carswell? Never. She hadn't been upstairs in years, since her health was too poor to make the climb. The detective? Unlikely. And detectives were trained to leave a room the way they found it. A new boarder? Perhaps. He may have entered my room by mistake. . . .I thought all of that in rapid succession, but I never thought that someone might still be in there until a shadow moved across the closed window shade. Then all rational thought left me. My heart pounded and I broke into a cold sweat. Should I run and call the cops? Should I hide in the bushes? Should I shinny up the drainpipe and peek in the window? No. It was my room. I paid the rent. I decided to take the bull by the horns and go upstairs . . . very carefully.

Ever so slowly, I opened the outside door to the stairwell

so it did not make any noise. The stairwell was pitch black
and I felt for the light switch and flicked it, but nothing
happened. There was no light at the top of the stairs, or in
the kitchen. I would have to go up in total dark. I took the
first two steps and then stopped and listened. Nothing. If
there was someone up there, he wasn't making any noise. I
took several more steps and, at about the middle of the
stairway, one of the old steps groaned as though it would
break and swallow my leg. Again I stopped and listened.
Whoever was up there must surely know I was there. I would
get trapped in that crypt of a stairwell, with the splinters of
a broken step driven deep into my ankle and holding me, so
the ghoul in my room could fly down and bash in my head.
But the step held and made little noise as I raised my foot,
and I made a mental note to skip it if I ever tried to sneak
in late at night with a girl. The other steps were not so creaky
and I finally made it to the top, where I had to turn right
and pass the open area of the kitchen to get to my room. The
ghoul could easily hide there and impale me on Mrs. Carswell's ten-inch bread knife as I passed. But a little moonlight
filtering in through a small window above the sink showed
me that the kitchen was empty. I crept along and, with no
sound at all, made it to my bedroom door. I could have kicked
it open, easily breaking the feeble lock. I could have caught
the intruder by surprise, pounced upon him, and disarmed
him with a flurry of punches like Mike Hammer. But I was
never so brave or so foolhardy, and I just bent down and
looked through the keyhole. To my astonishment, and great
relief, I could see that Jody was in there, lying on my bed.
My fear instantly subsided but my heartbeat stayed strong
as I twisted the knob and gently pushed open the door. She
smiled nervously and sat up, and I tried to act as though I
was used to finding girls on my bed at all hours of the night.

"What a pleasant surprise," I said.

"Did I scare you? You're as pale as a ghost."

"It's nothing," I shrugged, and paced the room to work off my nervous energy.

"I'll go." She stood up.

"No, it's just. . . ." I hadn't calmed down yet, and I didn't know what to say, so I kept on pacing.

"Maybe you were expecting someone else. A student, perhaps."

"I'm not in the habit of romancing my students." Her comment annoyed me at first, then I thought about Bonnie. I pictured her and Jody together, the open lustiness of one and the veiled sensuality of the other. Bonnie was the bawdy Wife of Bath, ready for action and willing to tell you so. But Jody, who appeared sober, steadfast, and demure as a Chaucerian nun, despite the gold amulet she wore with the inscription *omnia vincit amor*, was by far the most enticing.

I stopped pacing, sat down on the bed, and said, "Let's start over."

She sat next to me but folded her arms across her chest as though she were chilly. "You mind that I'm here, don't you," she said.

"I don't mind. I like it." I touched her elbow and she relaxed her arms. I smiled to think that I was apologizing for her being there and scaring me half to death. I was intrigued by how women could do that; how they could boldly enter your bedroom, lie wantonly on your bed, and then somehow make you feel like an intruder. It was a ritual I'd noticed, particularly among Southern women, to firmly establish beforehand that the male was making the advances, even if he was not. Don't get me wrong, though. I was pleased that Jody had again taken the initiative and did not mind if she conferred the credit upon me.

"By the way, how did you get in here?" I asked as though we'd just happened to meet in the park.

"That nice lady downstairs." She held up a passkey that Mrs. Carswell had given her. "I told her I was your sister."

If it were that simple, Cowpens's killer could have told Mrs. Carswell that he was my brother and she'd have let him in too. I felt more vulnerable than ever before.

"With security like this, it's a wonder there's any crime." I took the key from her, slipped it into my pocket, and made a mental note to tell Mrs. Carswell never to hand it out again . . . except to Jody.

"If you'd been home at a decent hour," she said, "I wouldn't have had to borrow the key."

"I was out with Carlos tonight." I looked at her carefully to see if there was any change in expression.

"Cruising chicks?" she asked blithely.

"We went to El Cid. Just a few drinks. Talking old times."

"Did you talk about me?"

"Constantly."

"You probably told him I chased after you at Elmer's Tradewinds, and you both had a good laugh."

"The Brazilian with the terrible temper, who just asked you to marry him? I'm not crazy, and we're no longer friends." I lay down on one elbow, and the springy old bed sunk in the middle and slid her toward me. She did not move away.

"It's me, isn't it," she said.

I nodded. "But we didn't talk about you. Not once. I don't know what's going through his mind . . . or yours." I rolled flat onto my back and put my hands behind my head. The bed came up in the middle and seemed to move her away.

"I'm in your bedroom, not his." She pursed her lips in her pretty, embarrassed way.

"Then you've told him you won't marry him?"

She shook her head. "I can't stand him at times, his insistence on my purity while he'd fuck anybody in town. I can't stand that, and that little dance he does whenever we're at a party."

"His samba?" I chuckled, but she was serious.

"I can't stand that he hates me, that he'll always hate me for having slept with you." She pursed her lips again and looked away.

"There ought to be a statute of limitations on jealousy." She wouldn't laugh, so I tried another equally unsuccessful line. "Brazilians only marry virgins, anyway."

"He thinks he'll be doing whoever he marries a favor," she said.

"Lucky he doesn't know about all the other guys you've had." I winked at her and she finally smiled. Then she lay down, hands behind her head like mine, and we looked at the ceiling.

"Did you bring him home to your parents?"

"You know what my father's like."

"Your mother too."

"Hush, now. If she knew I was in the bedroom of a Yankee, a divorced one at that, she'd have a fit."

"I'm not divorced."

"Will you be?" she asked coyly.

"It's in the works." It was a small lie since I was convinced my wife and I were finished for good.

"When will the divorce be final?"

"Don't you want anything to do with me until then?" I rolled onto my side and faced her. She turned her head and looked at me and, in one magic moment, our lips met in a warm, soft kiss. She thrust herself hard against me and trembled for all the lost years. I kissed her neck, and a wisp of her hair tickled my nose. Then I cupped one of her full, firm breasts and she moaned. Our clothes were off in a heartbeat, shed easier than Magnolia's Street's leaves in autumn. I touched the petals of her sweet sex and brushed her with my hardness. She moaned again, so ready, so wet.

She nibbled at my ear and to my puzzlement and delight whispered, "Vivamus, mea Lesbia . . . atque amemus. . . ."

"Catallus?"

"You remember."

I entered her slowly and she sighed. I had to be still or I would finish too fast. I wanted it to last more than the moment, and to recall all of our moments past. I wanted to be transported, to Mycenae and to Corinth. . . .

". . . soles occidere . . . et redire possunt . . ."

I wanted to reach the grand, golden solitude of sun-bleached temples that were surrounded by the wine-dark sea. . . .

". . . nobis cum semel . . . occidut breuis lux . . ."

"What does that mean?" I begged, but she wouldn't tell me, and more of her ancient love words gushed forth to echo their world of youth and beauty, of unencumbered frolic when time and the earth stood still. . . .

". . . nox est perpetua . . . una dormienda . . ."

Her warmth surrounded me and I was transported. I needed no translation at all.

We made love throughout the night, replenishing our long-lost ardor, fulfilling our urgent needs. Dawn found us asleep, entwined beneath my only blanket, two embraced as one, defying and defeating November's bleak chill. Such moments, though, too often fly and we were startled awake by a rude pounding on the bedroom door.

$\triangledown$

Chapter 15

THE DETECTIVE AND I sat in Mrs. Carswell's kitchen while Jody remained in the bedroom. He wore the same brown suit he'd had on when poking around Cowpens's room just after the murder. I wore only a bathrobe. My feet were bare and the floor was cold.

"Got a hot young coed in there, professor?" He nodded toward my room with a lecherous grin.

"None of your business," I snapped, and then realized that's the way the police sometimes work. They make you hostile and you slip and say something you don't want to, or they try the man-to-man approach, like a pal, and get you to spill your guts. I had to be careful.

"Between you and me," he said, "when I was first up here, I thought you were a fag."

"You have something important, officer, this early on a Sunday morning?"

"Not really," he said smugly. "Just that the fag who lived up here crashed his car."

"Is he hurt?"

"He's part of a pink smear on a bridge abutment."

The floor felt colder. I shivered and pulled my bathrobe tighter around me.

"Whadda you care? I can see you ain't a faggot." He grinned and looked toward my room again.

"I don't believe it. . . ." I referred to his callousness, not to Warren's death, but he didn't get, or chose to ignore, my drift.

"Pity about the car," he said. "Little pink T'bird. Musta thought he was Richard Petty . . . or Richard Pretty." He laughed. I didn't. "He was going fast, over a hundred. Of course they couldn't tell from the speedometer, since they had to dig his face out of it."

"That's enough!"

"Easy, professor. Like I said, whadda you care?"

"He was a nice man."

"Nice?" He winced. "He was arrested fifty times for drunk driving, disorderly conduct, public lewdness, and you name it. And that's the best we could do since the days when you could lock up fags like him and throw away the key."

"I only met him a few times up here and he was no problem." I stared at him, determined to put in a good word.

"Obviously, you've been too busy"—he indicated my room again—"or he'd have been after your ass."

"I don't have to worry now, do I."

"You're losing roommates pretty quick." He raised one eyebrow. "Just you up here now, isn't it?"

"No more queers and old rednecks."

"Hah! You liberal professors." He got up from his chair and started to leave, but he stopped at the head of the stairwell.

"Be careful." He held up a forefinger. "You're the third one up here, and you know what they say about bad luck in threes, and three on a match."

"And thank God none of us match, officer."

"You liberal professors." He shook his head and turned and started down the stairs.

"Was he drinking?" I called out, and he stopped.

"Dead-cold sober," he shouted back up the stairwell. "Musta been asleep." He thumped down the stairs and was gone.

Asleep? I thought I knew better, that he was distraught over Cowpens's murder. Or perhaps he knew about the stone and was upset that he didn't get it. Or maybe someone knew that he knew and rigged the car to go off the road. . . . Before my imagination ran completely away with me, I went back to my room and slipped into bed with Jody.

"Your feet are cold," she said. "I'll warm them . . . but you only if you tell me why the police are after you."

I told her about Warren crashing into the bridge abutment, but omitted the gory details the detective had used. I also told her that he and Cowpens Martin had been the best of friends.

"The dead man at Elmer's Tradewinds? That awful little man who lived with you?"

"He wasn't awful and he lived at this rooming house, not with me."

"Creepy." She snuggled next to me. "I was up here all alone waiting for you . . . among all these . . . ghosts."

Her feet warmed mine and I drifted off into a half-sleep that was troubled by the ghosts of the past; the nasty, straggling ectoplasm that never dies, the small reminders and quirks of an earlier life as seen in the mannerisms and expressions one has learned from a former companion or lover. Jody had a few she'd gained from Carlos, which she used comfortably and subconsciously from her long association with him. One little phrase that was his, "I have my ways," she used quite often and, though I couldn't resent it, it rankled. Perhaps such reminders were part of the price I had to pay for leaving her as I did, so he could move in like a piranha and teach her his ways. I considered her lucky, though, since she had never known my wife and could not identify the little phrases and foibles I'd picked up from her and be rankled.

As I lay there, on the brink between wakefulness and sleep, I gradually became content to be again so close to Jody. The rankling little ghosts slipped quietly away, and I even forgot the big important issues of Cowpens, Warren, and the rock. But when we got out of bed almost an hour later to take a bath together in Mrs. Carswell's big old tub, they all came back to haunt me.

"Is this your private bathroom?" Jody asked as we gingerly sat down facing each other in the hot water. "Or did 'they' use it?"

"They? You mean the dead guys?"

She nodded but looked down at the water, seemingly afraid to touch it with her hands.

"They weren't here much." I thought of the ring Cowpens would have left from all the dirt picked up out with the road crew, and of the scented bubble bath Warren probably used. I imagined them clean, relaxed, and alive in that tub, as we were, and I smiled, and Jody relaxed too.

She shifted her long legs around me to get more comfortable. Then she produced a rubber band from nowhere and secured her lengths of wispy brown hair in a loose arrangement atop her head. I watched her slender arms and fingers move gracefully, and the old bathroom became steam-filled and exotic. The plumbing fixtures behind her, which harbored a green mould from the constant moisture, became part of some ancient Greek statuary encrusted with verdigris. The chipped old porcelain tub became a huge oyster's half-shell, and she was Venus rising from the sea. I formed a goblet with my hands and scooped warm water onto her breasts. Then I soaped them, and felt their incredible slipperiness and gently kneaded their rubbery firmness. I marveled at how white they were, at their thin, nearly transparent skin and the blue serpentine veins that showed through in such a delicate pattern. And they were very big for such a slender girl. Her nipples were dark in comparison, puckered and thick, a remarkable contrast.

"I'd like to soap these up on national television, in a commercial," I said, "and announce that you're my Ivory Girl."

"I'd like that." She giggled, sat up straight, and thrust her perfect orbs out even more.

"Up periscope," I announced as my aroused manhood broke the water's surface.

"I like your submarine, or is it a torpedo?" She grasped hold with both hands and soaped it squeaky clean. We washed and played until the water cooled and the steam disappeared, so the place again became a bathroom that Cowpens and Warren had used. Then, slipping and clutching each other for balance, we got out of the tub and patted each other dry with my only towel.

"If you're expecting a monogram," I said, "forget it."

"But it's got one." She showed me where the towel was stamped *Sutherland College Student Linen Service*.

"Now you know why the detective was really here this morning." We laughed and dressed and went out to get some breakfast.

The morning air was crisp and clear, and the remnant of a frost disappeared from shaded hiding places as the sun rose toward noon. I had parked my car directly behind Jody's, and now kicked myself for not realizing it was hers. I'd seen it outside Carlos's house the night she dropped in, outside

Elmer's after Cowpens was killed. Some detective I was. I could have saved myself a lot of anxiety and fear. We took my car, however, and had to sit a moment while the old engine warmed up.

"Do you want a restaurant outside of town, so we don't run into Carlos?"

"He doesn't own me. Besides, he's always home at this hour on Sunday morning."

"You know his habits well."

"You care?"

The cold light of day had set a new scene, and reminded me that ghosts also appear in the sunshine.

"I don't own you, either," I said. "But the thought has crossed my mind." I wanted the magic to continue.

"You mean that?" She threw her arms around me.

"I mean, the thought has crossed my mind."

She pretended to pout and then put her head on my shoulder and hugged me. "If you leave me again, please tell me, this time, before you go."

"I deeply regretted how callous I'd once been, how I'd left without telling her and only called after I reached New York. At least I had never lied to her about my intentions and, though I wanted to assure her, I would not lie to her now. Lucky for me, the Tempest's engine had warmed to a throaty purr and, without another word, I pulled out into the quiet, empty streets of Sutherland.

In less than a mile, we passed big, gleaming-white Central Methodist and saw the churchgoers file in. Farther on, at the outskirts of town, we saw a line of black people entering a modest but proud old Baptist church. It was a typical Southern Sunday morning, like all the ones I recalled from my undergraduate days, when the studiers had been up and were already marching toward the library, the jocks and the fitness buffs were out turning a few laps, the hell-raisers were still sleeping off their hangovers, and the pious were shuffling into their pews. The South hadn't changed and it wouldn't: the whites still owned Central Methodist and the blacks had ramshackle Baptist on the outskirts of town.

Eventually we stopped at a restaurant called Simple Simon's, and I was certain it had been named after the waitresses. They scrambled our order more thoroughly than the eggs, and the addition of our check required a consultation among the entire staff that brought more perplexed expressions than I'd seen in a dozen of my Middle English classes.

"You add it up for them," I said to Jody as I shoveled in my food and she played with hers.

"Not on your life," she said. "I teach Latin, not math."

"Latin is very mathematical."

"How so?"

"The Roman numerals are pretty famous."

"Very funny, but there were some great mathematicians in Roman times."

"Catullus?"

"He was a poet, silly. A very erotic poet, as you know."

"I know," I whispered across the table, hoping the onions in my hash browns would not offend her. "I like it when you recite to me, when we make love." I reached out and held her hand.

"I like it when you hold hands with me," she said. "You never used to."

"I'm different now."

"But the same."

"Yes, but I've learned some things."

"Carlos wouldn't hold hands with me, either. I was beginning to wonder."

"They're pretty," I admired her long, slender fingers and nicely shaped nails that were free of polish.

"I don't mean that he didn't like them. I mean you can tell how much a guy likes you if he holds your hand in public."

"Shows commitment, I guess."

"More than a ring."

"That means whoever marries who doesn't need to buy a ring. He just needs to hold your hand a lot."

"I didn't say that."

One of the waitresses finally brought our checks, torn and full of erasures.

"Can I deduct for lack of neatness?" I asked.

"It's just a check," she drawled, annoyed. "You can check it if you want."

"I was only kidding. I'm an English teacher. You remember how you always asked your teacher if neatness counts?"

"Well, it's just a check," she repeated, impatient and unamused. She walked back to her coffee station, where she whispered with some of the other waitresses and occasionally threw a hostile look in my direction.

"They're not interested in your Yankee humor down here," Jody told me.

"I don't know. If I had a drawl, she'd be rolling in the aisles. I think she likes me. She keeps looking over here."

"She's just making sure you don't leave without paying."

"You think?" I used one of Jody's favorite expressions, in my best Southern drawl.

"I think." She smiled and squeezed my hand.

"You know, when I first came back here I felt I was in a foreign land."

"And now you feel at home?"

"No. Now I have an interpreter."

We laughed and, without checking for errors or discounting for lack of neatness, I paid the check. Outside, in Simple Simon's parking lot, we could see the Blue Ridge Mountains lying long and low in their veil of mist.

"They really are blue," I said as I scanned the Paleozoic crinkle that runs from Maine to Georgia.

"Your eyes?" Jody looked only at me.

I turned to her and looked into her eyes, and put my arms around her waist. We kissed. It was a long, soft, moist kiss that was veiled in mist and love's mystery, like the Blue Ridge Wall. And like that very old block of stone, which weather and running water had carved into sharp ravines and jagged peaks so it looked younger than its hundreds of millions of years, Jody and I were young again. She was a freshman and I was a senior and our love, once worn flat and nearly dissolved by distance and time, was being reshaped and renewed by colossal forces beyond our control. We'd been battered and humbled, like the mountain chain before us, but maybe we had another chance.

"Let's go there," I said when we broke the kiss.

"To the mountains?"

"To look around."

I don't know if she shared my enthusiasm for geology, but she certainly wanted to go up there. We climbed into my Tempest and rolled up Interstate 26. Soon the big road's four broad lanes ended, cut off as though confounded by the mighty Blue Ridge Wall. I liked to think that nature had stopped man there, that the crusty old earth had thrown up an impenetrable barrier, that there were places where we could not and should not go, that man can never entirely gird the earth in concrete. I'd thought that about the moon once too—that we couldn't and shouldn't go there—and I knew the reason we'd made it was the same reason that

Interstate 26 could not make it over the Blue Ridge Wall. Money. But the highway department would have enough of that someday and they'd finish. Their machines would come back, their giant dozers and great crawling Caterpillars, and they'd grind the ground and snort their noxious fumes, and leave their residue of concrete like so much caterpillar slime. That day, however, I was pleased to think it was easier to get to the moon than it was to get Interstate 26 up and over the mighty Blue Ridge Wall.

The interstate dumped off into an old two-laner, a winding, precipitous piece of blacktop that doubled back on itself a hundred times in its slow, tortuous climb along the harsh contours of the steepest grade east of the Mississippi. It was a poor road but it was pretty, going only where nature allowed it. As such, it was subject to closures from rockslides, snow, and ice. The most powerful cars and tractor trailers were humbled by its steepness. On that day, however, with Jody, my little Tempest took it in stride. We passed through little towns like East Flatrock, Fletcher, and Skyland, and saw a sign for Carl Sandburg's home, a minor tourist attraction that was best seen in a warmer month for perfume, color, and sweetness of remembrance.

At first, the way was deceptively soft, the rocks moss-covered, pine-strewn, and buffed smooth by millions of years of weathering. The water seeped, rather than gushed, from between the cracks in the mountainside. But the climb suddenly steepened and the gentle roller coaster ride became a hard pull. The friendly towns and mellow waterways vanished and only low, weak walls of stone and cement would keep us from disaster if I miscalculated, or skidded, or swerved to avoid an animal or another car. We swept through a hairpin curve slightly faster than I'd planned, and Jody's pretty knuckles grew white on the door handle, but she said nothing. Ah, young love. My wife would have screamed and called me a jerk—I wondered why love eroded so much more quickly than the mountains. At one point we had to slow behind a car pulling a trailer. It seemed they'd never make it up the grade. I imagined a balding man at the wheel, wife nagging, children screaming. I also imagined he'd like to stow them all in the trailer and pull the pin, setting them free to find eternity in the six-thousand-foot drop down to the Piedmont. I thought of how my wife had pulled the pin on me, and then I wanted to help him, to push him with my Tempest to the top of the mountain. But I only passed him at the first chance and let him eat my dust.

Within a mile or two, we whisked by what I thought was the turnoff for roadcut 42. I had almost forgotten it during the climb. It was down a narrow side road, nearly hidden by foliage, marked only a low, wooden milepost with the same number I'd seen on the country's surveyor's map in the Sutherland College library. There was no point in stopping to look at a bunch of rocks, and I wouldn't have known a rough diamond if I tripped on it. But I made a mental note of where the side road was, in case I had to go with The Rock, and I must have done a double take as we shot past.

"What's wrong?" asked Jody.

"Thought I saw a deer, off in the woods."

"That's wonderful. City boy flies off steep mountain road, looking at deer."

"We have deer in New York—"

"Look at the road." Her words sounded more like caring advice than criticism, and she touched my thigh so it felt good. I looked at the road.

Finally, triumphantly, we reached the top of Blue Ridge Wall and rode the plateau to Asheville, North Carolina. I knew only that Asheville was a resort town, a summer retreat for Floridians seeking the cool mountain air, and I had no idea what Jody and I would do there in November, except ride around and take in the scenery before heading back down the treacherous mountainside to Sutherland. However, we soon noticed a roadsign for the Biltmore House, on the outskirts of Asheville, and Jody told me she'd never seen it and would like to go.

"Big mansion," I said. "French renaissance, or something. Largest private residence in North America, or someplace."

"You're not much of a tour guide."

"I was there sixteen years ago. Forgot the facts, except that there are two hundred and fifty rooms."

"That's impressive to me but, if it bores you, don't let's go on my account." She spoke sincerely, and I liked it. My wife would have dragged me there at any cost.

"No, no. There are a lot of things in the South worth seeing twice. At least every sixteen years."

"Very funny, but I don't want to go if you're going to make fun."

I apologized and told her it was most impressive by any standard, and I also wanted to go. We followed some more signs that directed us to the gatehouse where we stopped and I paid an admission fee that had grown quite substantial since the days when I'd last been there. Then we drove up the three-mile driveway to the main house. The road meandered through a pleasant wood, rising as it went, and finally emptied onto a giant open courtyard, across which loomed the huge and magnificent Biltmore House. It puts Yates Sutherland's house into perspective as a dwarf and, of course, as a monument to everything tacky. It had taken a thousand workmen five years to construct it in the 1890's for a grandson of Cornelius Vanderbilt. The house served as his summer retreat, with lavish formal gardens and a hunting preserve that ran for thousands of acres through the then virgin forest. I parked. There were few other cars in the offseason, and Jody and I stepped out onto the courtyard, where we beheld what seemed a view of the entire Appalachian Mountain chain.

"I never imagined it was so grand," she said, skipping as she took my hand and pulled me across the courtyard to the front door. When we got to the thick, oaken front door, we found it wide open and unprotected by attendants or guards. We entered unchallenged and I chuckled to think it was tougher to get by Mrs. Carswell, or the old college librarian. We stood in the entrance hall and looked around, and went back a hundred years.

"Now that's an arras." I noted a heavy, richly embroidered tapestry that adorned an entire wall. "I can see how Polonius might die behind something like that and not be discovered until they smelled him."

"Cheerful thought. Why don't you pull it down for show-and-tell in your Shakespeare class."

"I don't even kiss and tell." I squeezed her hand.

"I do," she teased, and squeezed back.

"Who're you going to tell?"

"My roommate, maybe." She shared her apartment with a girl who worked at the Citizen's Southern Bank.

"Is that because she's a teller?"

"Ooh. That pun is so bad the guards are coming for you." A uniformed man shuffled toward us from a dark, wood-paneled corner of the hall and told us we could wait for the next tour to start in twenty-five minutes, or we could wander around on our own since there were so few people in the building. We decided to wander and took in the main floor, where we gaped at the seventy-foot ceiling in the banquet hall and admired the three fireplaces, among more than sixty in the house. We looked at stenciled ceilings, linenfold paneling and artwork by Whistler, Renoir, and Durer. When we'd had our fill of all the carved wood, limestone, and marble, we went upstairs and found the master bedroom, which had an ornate pedestal bed surrounded by floor stanchions with velvet ropes.

"You think they put those up so we can't jump on and have a go at it?" I asked.

"I think," she said demurely, "people do some strange things."

"Making love is strange?"

"No, silly, but climbing on the Vanderbilt's bed . . ."

"Come on." I playfully unhooked one of the velvet ropes. "We're the only ones here."

"And you'll be the only one on that bed," she scolded, but her eyes told me we'd be wrapped in passion if it were my bed back at Mrs. Carswell's. Still, I tugged her toward the big bed.

She pulled away. "Someone will come."

"Talk about bad puns." I let her go and replaced the rope. We continued our tour through more opulent bedrooms, and were allowed to peek into some obscenely large baths and a few cavernous closets that could have held my paltry wardrobe a hundred times over. We agreed it would be nice to have that kind of wealth, but it was an empty agreement. It was only conversation that let us reestablish contact with reality in that fantasy setting. When we'd finished seeing the place, we were glad to be again outside.

It was cold in the courtyard and rapidly growing dark, and Jody huddled against me as we walked to the car.

"I wish this were our house," she said, "and we lived here alone."

"But the heating bill. And who would cut the lawn?"

She smiled. She'd expected a flip answer. She wasn't hurt, and the fact that I wouldn't grind out the early spark of love under heavy words of commitment somehow reassured her.

$\triangledown$

Chapter 16

F RESHMAN ENGLISH, MONDAY MORNING. I had not prepared a lecture and, worse, I was not prepared to face Bonnie
Weber. She was back, sitting front row, center as usual, and
the moment I walked in I felt she'd read me more closely
than the assignment. It was worse than the Monday morning after Yates Sutherland's party, when she had stripped
me naked in front of my class. I tried not to look at her as I
rummaged in my briefcase for the textbook, laid it open on
the lectern and gave my total unpreparedness away by asking
them where we'd left off.

One of the eggheads quickly raised his hand and said, "We
were getting to the meat of Pound, sir."

"You were pounding your meat," called a football player
from the back of the room.

The class burst into laughter, but I managed to keep a
straight face and tried to restore order by immediately asking
the football player what he knew about Ezra Pound. He
mumbled that he knew little or nothing, though he'd read
what I'd assigned, and had concluded that no one could
understand him or should bother to try. The class laughed
again and I frowned to show my displeasure, then let the
egghead discourse on the subject. His comments seemed

astute and I did not challenge him, for I tended to agree with the football player, and I had not read Pound since my student days in Freshman, English.

As the egghead went on, I went off into dreamland. My weekend with Jody was still too fresh and real for me to cast myself into the dry dreams and longings of the dead poets and writers in the Norton Anthology. I wished I could be with her at that moment, that I could sit invisible in her Latin class at Sutherland High and watch her steeped in conjugation. I wanted to escape, the way an old professor of mine used to do after a big night with the bottle. Red-faced and bleary-eyed, he'd put his head down on the desk and lament, "I can't go on," and dismiss us. I wouldn't do it, though. They'd paid for an hour of my time and I had to give them the quid pro quo. . . .

Suddenly the egghead stopped and I feared I would have to step in, but a discussion was sparked among several of them, which I let continue. I could take advantage, I thought, and let the thing escalate into a bullshit session that would use up the whole hour. I was lucky. The poor math professors had to give real, finite answers, though they could occasionally throw up a long equation on the blackboard and work it for days. History professors had it rough too, in that they had to open their text every day and sustain their neverending march through the chronology of purportedly significant events therein. But the physics professors had it best. They could describe the physical nature of the universe in grand theories and dazzle you with measurements in terms of the speed of light, or write equations on the blackboard that ran from here to eternity. And it was all too complex for their students to challenge, whereas any of my students would think nothing of telling me that Dos Passos was too long-winded and that Hemingway would have a tough time getting published today. My universe could not match that of the physics professors, nor could I equal their arrogance. For I was certain that only God and poets had the real equations to rightly describe the universe. Yet if, when they graduated, my students knew only that they knew nothing, they'd come out ahead. They'd know more than the business majors, who thought they knew it all—for whom liberal arts was an anachronism. Their legend and lore was the CRT database and some fast-forgotten scoundrels who managed to run up a quick score on Wall Street.

As the egghead spoke on, I tried not to look at Bonnie. Her presence disturbed me, but not as much as the fact that I had nothing to tell my class. So, I joined in their discourse, which led into a lecture, and I found myself totally absorbed and sweating when Old Main's bell tower signaled the end of the period. It was only then that I noticed I'd removed my jacket and rolled up my shirt-sleeves. I was proud that I'd avoided the maudlin, head-on-the-desk dismissal, and that I'd pulled out all the stops and rolled out all of English Literature's nuts and bolts that time would allow. And the class was pleased, I thought, especially since the football players had not formed their usual flying wedge for the door. In fact, they sat perfectly still as I drove home my final point, slapped the textbook shut, and waved them away.

Only Bonnie remained while I rolled my shirt-sleeves back down and replaced my jacket. And with all the thunder and lightning I'd so masterfully thrown at the class, I did not know what to say to the lone coed. I wanted to go, but her green eyes latched onto mine. I tried to look away, but there were only the dull, unadorned classroom walls. She drew me back into her gaze, to her smile, and to her soft cotton shirt with her proud breasts free and jutting underneath. Keep cool, I told myself. Keep cool, and be honest.

"Going to the canteen?" she asked. I shook my head and

she said, "Buy you a cup of coffee?"

"No, thanks."

"Or a Pepsi. In the bottle. And you can pour peanuts down the neck."

"No. But sit down. I want to talk to you a minute."

"I'm sorry I missed class last week." She pretended to pout. "You know how it is. When the Charleston Symphony whispers low, thou must—"

"That's not it."

"Oh, professor, you didn't like my morality tale."

"No, I liked it. Very much. And I like you. You're very attractive and, uh, the only one in class who can pronounce Middle English so it doesn't sound like Gullah."

"Thanks a lot."

"And then there's, ah . . ."

"What, professor? You can tell me."

"I'm seeing someone else." There. I'd said it. I'd ended our flirtation in one sentence, and I was prepared for anger, or tears, but not her response.

"That's great," she said, genuinely pleased. "Me too. That's why I didn't make it to Elmer's Tradewinds that night. I hope you're not mad."

"Oh . . . of course not." I was relieved, though disillusioned by my own imagination. She was teaching me now, and the lesson was well taken.

She moved toward the door and then stopped, ready to tell me something more. I'll never know what it was because the Rock brushed by her just then and entered. She went out and shut the door.

"It's a diamond, lad," he said when he was certain we were the only ones in the room. "It's a diamond," he repeated, and it's as big as a house."

$\triangledown$

Chapter 17

IT HAD BEEN A week since I'd left Cowpens's stone with The Rock. Just after I'd given it to him, he explained, he got an emergency call from an oil-drilling site in Louisiana that had come up dry. He'd flown there immediately to consult with other petroleum geologists on whether to drill further or abandon the site. He'd had to stay there a week and had only gotten to examine the stone when he returned on Sunday night. I did not ask him, nor did I care, if he'd found any oil.

"And it's really a diamond?" I was still shocked, and disbelieving.

"Had to clean it first. Solution of hydrochloric acid. Then I slipped it under the old electron microscope . . ."

A student threw open the door and barged in past The Rock and me without saying a word. He clamored through a row of chairs, dropping his pencils and several books, and finally slumped into his seat, where he looked a lot less than bright and ready for his next class. I was about to snap at him for the rude interruption, but The Rock, noticing my annoyance, winked at me and said, "The thirst for education is a powerful one, lad." He nodded toward the door. I gathered my notes and books into my briefcase and we walked out.

"It's marvelous." The Rock's eyes sparkled like diamonds as we hit the sunlight outside Old Main and strolled together across the campus. "Clear as a bell, and not a speck of carbon."

"Carbon?"

"Diamonds are formed from it, under great pressure. When they're not perfect, they retain bits of the black stuff and it diminishes their value."

I could see he was excited. His cheeks were rosy and he sustained a smile that made the laugh lines around his eyes very deep.

"Then it's valuable?" I asked foolishly, knowing diamonds were valuable of course but wanting to be assured.

"Don't know the market value, rough or otherwise, lad, but one this size should be worth a considerable sum." Visions of wealth danced in my head, but his thoughts were elsewhere. "It's the find, though, not the worth," he continued. "It's a geological phenomenon that'll mean international acclaim."

"I don't need that."

"Money, huh? Don't blame you but, personally, I'd rather be known for the find."

"You're already known for finding oil."

"Oh, I tell 'em where the huge reservoirs are, or should be, but that's not the same. Do you realize what you've got here? It can be tough enough to find a golf ball on a par-three hole at the Sutherland Country Club, let alone a golf ball-sized diamond on this great continent."

"I never thought of it that way."

"A stone like this can make you immortal. Collectors'll pay far beyond its market value just to own the largest diamond ever found in North America. In fact, some collectors might not bother to pay for it, if you know what I mean."

He stopped smiling, though the sparkle was still in his eyes, and my ecstatic dreams of wealth sank into sordid thoughts of the dead Cowpens Martin. He could have been the start of a long, cursed history, like that of the Hope Diamond, and I could find immortality far sooner than I'd bargained.

"I'm not a collector of anything," I said. "I'll sell it as soon as possible and disavow any association with it."

"But you should be proud, lad."

"If you'd found it, you'd probably have earned it through painstaking investigation and the application of revolutionary geological principles, or something, and you'd probably write a book. I'm just a blind hog who rooted up an acorn."

He grasped hold of my arm and stopped us from walking. "We're all just blind hogs, lad. But, if we root around enough, we develop a sixth sense for those acorns."

"And that's called 'genius,' if I remember your lectures."

"Indeed it is." He grinned and brought fifty more laugh lines back to his face. He let go of my arm and we continued toward his office in the oldest dormitory on campus.

"What intrigues me, though," he said offhandedly, "is that you found the stone in a car. Pink, wasn't it?" I had mentioned the pink T'bird as a joke when I first brought it to him, but then I'd told him I found it at a roadcut. I wondered if he'd forgotten or if he was testing me for some reason.

"I was only kidding," I said.

"Of course. It was a roadcut. I remember. And where did you say it was?"

I hadn't told him the location or that it was number 42, as Cowpens had written in his note. I suppose I could have picked any old roadcut but I feared that too many lies might trap me.

"It's in the mountains," I said, "where my car overheated . . . bad water pump . . ."

"You told me that too, I believe. But where?" Suddenly, his memory was too good. It put me on guard, and I proceeded with caution.

"I can find it again, I'm sure. I wasn't paying much attention. I was worried about getting water for my car." I felt clever to emphasize the water pump, since I had the repair bill to corroborate that part of the story. I wanted to build a case that established the stone as mine, though I did feel guilty that Cowpens would get none of the money or credit.

"Can you take me there?" he asked as we entered the dormitory and started down the narrow stairs to the basement. I pretended to concentrate on navigating the steps, while I considered whether or not I should take him out to roadcut 42. We reached his office at the bottom of the stairwell and I stood aside for him to open the door. He put his hand on the knob but didn't turn it. He just looked at me, waiting for an answer to his question.

"I can take you," I said. "Do you think there are any more diamonds?"

"Unlikely, lad, but anything's possible. I've looked around the Carolinas myself, in areas adjacent to volcanic tubes. I've even found a couple, but they were puny. Not even industrial quality. Worthless." He twisted the knob, shoved the door open, and continued talking as we went into his office and he sat down behind his desk. "The conditions are right for diamonds to have gotten here, but the region's so old that everything has been worn down and washed all over the place. Still, I'd like to see that roadcut."

"My last class is at two, and we can split whatever we find." I sat on the chair in front of his desk.

"Don't need money, lad." He chuckled as he took out his pipe and lit up.

"Then you take all the credit and I'll take all the money." We laughed, realizing we were both selfish children who coveted what we considered the best toys and grudgingly meted out the others to our playmates.

"By the way," I asked as casually as I could, "where is the stone now?"

"In here." He puffed his pipe and waved his hand around the office.

"But the door wasn't locked!" I was on the edge of panic.

"Never is."

"I know. But it's been in here for a week?" I began to regret all the nice things I'd said about him—his unique method of teaching and his open-door policy—and to think he was a fool.

"Don't worry, lad. It's hidden in plain sight." He grinned mischievously and I glanced around at the trays of rocks that ringed the small room. There were hundreds of them, all carefully labeled: pyrite, bauxite, malachite, sial. . . .His desk was strewn with rocks, several of which could have been the diamond, but I wasn't sure. If it was another test, I had certainly failed.

"You mean I could hand you a mere piece of quartz and keep your precious stone for myself?" He studied my perplexed look.

"You could. . . ." I had to go along with his little game. Then I realized he'd given me a clue. I scanned the trays again and went over to the one labeled *quartzite*. I picked it up and poked through the rocks in it, but none looked like mine. They were, for the most part, close to the size of mine but they had no dark crud on them as mine had.

"Look closer, lad."

I probed some more and finally noticed one stone that was, from certain angles, crystal clear. I held it up to the light and squinted, but it still looked like quartz to me.

"They're prettier when they're cut and polished," he said, "and the light reflects off all the facets."

"You're sure. . . ."

"That's it, lad. Take it. It's yours."

I examined it some more and then shrugged and put it into the side pocket of my jacket. It made a pretty good lump there and I patted it through the cloth, uncertain that it was as safe as it had been in the tray of quartz. I thanked The Rock and, as I turned to go, he warned, "Don't tell anyone yet. You'll start a stampede to that roadcut and all the evidence will be destroyed."

"And all the other diamonds will be gone," I playfully added. He chuckled some more and puffed his pipe, and I went off to my next class. I would follow his advice and not tell anyone, so that he could play Sherlock Holmes and look unencumbered for great geological clues. And maybe we would find more diamonds. His use of the word *evidence* bothered me though, with Cowpens's death and my guilt over taking his stone. I wondered who else he had told about it and if, when the world found out, the object of my guilt and greed, that little lump in my pocket, would only turn out to be evidence that could put me in jail for murder.

My remaining lectures were a shambles. For the rest of the day I thought only of the diamond and constantly patted the lump in my jacket to make sure it was still there. I feared that my students would think me crazy. I tried to stay calm, but my gestures became wild and my writing on the blackboard turned into a frenzied scrawl that no one could read. They looked at me as though nothing were different, and I felt like Poe's madman in "The Telltale Heart" who'd murdered an old man and, when the detectives came, ranted and raved to cover up the sound of the old man's heartbeat that grew ever louder inside his head. It seemed the rock in my pocket had a life of its own, a heartbeat that would tip off the young detectives before me to the fact that I'd taken a murdered old man's treasure. Thump, thump, thump, the dead rock beat in my jacket and I, like a fool or a madman, patted it again to make sure it was there.

My class could not end fast enough. When the bell finally rang, I beat my students out the door and dashed across the campus to The Rock's office.

▽

Chapter 18

W E TOOK THE ROCK'S new Buick so I could look for the roadcut while he drove. On the way, he pointed out some of the more remarkable features of the Piedmont, giving me a refresher course in the local geology. Within a half hour we had reached the mighty Blue Ridge Wall, where the interstate stopped and we were routed onto the twisty two-laner up the Saluda Grade toward Asheville. As the big Buick climbed, The Rock shifted his dissertation from the flat Piedmont to the forming of the mountains.

"Just a wrinkle in the earth's crust, lad, and we're presented with a thousand miles of mountain from Maine to Georgia."

"Plate tectonics, right?"

"See that motel?" He ignored me as we passed a small motel that was nestled in a space cut into the mountainside. "Someday that mountain's going to come down on top of it. I stop in every once in a while and tell the owner, but he only laughs. He doesn't seem to understand that that much rock and dirt can't sit at such a steep angle for very long."

"Living under the sword of Damocles." I had to bring it into my discipline.

"Precisely, lad. It could slide down on top of him tomorrow

. . . or it could happen in two thousand years. When it goes, though, it'll sweep that little motel right across this road and down into the river valley on the other side."

"He must be betting it'll take two thousand years," I said.

"I'm betting different. There's plenty of mica in this soil. That's slippery, you know. They make talcum powder out of it. And when the face of that mountain reaches its shear point, I'll be glad I didn't book a room."

"Or ride by it," I added as the Buick swept around a curve and climbed some more, and the motel was gone from view.

"People don't understand the volatile nature of this planet, lad. They think its core is solid iron, not molten, and that its crust is immovable bedrock that will last a billion years. They also think that the trees and plants are here to stay, and that the breathable air and the sweet rain will never leave us. But this is an old planet, and it's run a very long course."

"And we're not helping it much, either."

"Precisely, lad. Considering the long history of the earth against the probable length of its future, we're standing at the abyss, looking over the edge."

"Well, I won't book a room in that motel, either." I tried to lighten the tone of our conversation. I must admit that, though I've always been concerned about the environment, I was more concerned about surviving from day to day.

"I don't mean to sound like a prophet of doom," he said. "This is a marvelous world, but we must understand its delicate systems better and work harder to sustain them."

The Buick's engine pinged on the steeper climbs, and I supposed that The Rock condoned low-octane unleaded gasoline and catalytic converters. He became silent as he concentrated on the winding road, while I looked out for the way to roadcut 42.

In a few miles, as we neared the top of the Blue Ridge Wall, where I'd passed before with Jody, I spotted the turnoff. I was about to tell him, but before I could speak he veered off onto the narrow little sideroad without even slowing down.

"You know where you're going?"

"Been here many times, lad." It was no longer my show. The Buick and he pulled me along like a landslide; irresistible, unstoppable. I trusted him, I thought, but I knew that diamonds could do strange things to people.

Soon, the sideroad turned into a rutted dirt path, thick with mud and puddles that remained from the weekend's heavy rain. The Buick slalomed along, its new springs and shocks making a squishy sound and its overstuffed velvet seats cushioning what the suspension couldn't handle. Dense foliage lined the path and scraped the car's shiny sides. The noise was agonizing to me, like broken chalk on a blackboard. The Rock noticed I was bothered but told me it couldn't be helped since the vehicle was dedicated to the interests of science.

"You need a Land Rover," I told him.

"Had one, once." He fishtailed out of a very deep rut and almost hit a tree, but whipped the wheel in the direction of the skid and regained control. "Buick beats it, though. These babies'll plow through anything, long as you keep up the momentum."

I laughed nervously, certain we'd slide off the road into the woods. I breathed a sigh a relief when we finally emerged from the dirt path into a small clearing and stopped. The sight before us was magnificent. We overlooked the Green River Gorge and the interstate highway bridge that spanned it—the bridge that was not yet connected to the interstate and seemed to begin and lead to nowhere.

"Marvelous, isn't it, lad? Just a big white concrete sculpture standing out there in space."

"I thought they built highways right up to where the bridges were to be and then spanned the chasms."

"They'll connect it, someday . . . and then the majesty of the place will be forgotten with the cars going by so fast."

"I wish it weren't here."

"Actually, lad, it makes the gorge look more awesome. Those gigantic pillars disappears down into the abyss, and that concrete slab on top seems to run off into infinity."

"I'd still like it better without it."

"It's not hurting anything now." He popped open his door and hopped out, and I did the same. "Man needs monuments to his ability," he said over the Buick's mud-covered hood.

"But you teach that man needs humility, not monuments to himself."

"True, but there's a balance here." He looked off across the gorge. "The earth has to give sometimes, and so do we."

"What have we given here?"

"Nothing, but we haven't really detracted. Sometimes that's the best we can do." He walked off, down a small slope toward the bridge, and I followed. He was in his element, sauntering, alert, and sniffing the air as though clues to the kinds of rocks he sought were carried on the wind. He donned a pair of work gloves as we covered the hundred yards or so to the edge of the gorge. For the first time, I noticed that he carried a mason's hammer that dangled from a piece of rawhide looped around his wrist. He strode out onto the bridge and I followed, aware of how very wide the gorge was and how sharply its side dropped off toward the Green River far below. When we reached the center of the span, he leaned perilously over the waist-high railing and looked down.

"Four hundred feet, lad."

I stood next to him, with two hands firmly on the rail, and also looked down. We were absorbed for a moment in the huge swell of concrete and space, and the only sounds we heard were the cold breeze through the naked trees and the icy rush of water that echoed up from the river, which was swollen from the recent rain. I bravely took one hand off the rail and slipped it into my jacket to touch the diamond. It was colder than the November wind that swept through the gorge. It had cooled for at least a million years, so many miles removed from the molten fire at the earth's core that had spawned it. I understood then why they call diamonds "ice." It's not because of their crystalline forms, but because they're so damned cold.

"I'm pretty sure you didn't find it up here on the bridge." The Rock snapped me back to reality.

"Down there." I removed my hand from my pocket and pointed at the river.

"That's a long way to go for an overheated car." He was right, of course. It would have been foolish to make such a difficult descent for water when there were probably other sources up where we were.

"I was overheated after I climbed back up." I tossed out a flip answer, hoping he wouldn't challenge me further.

"Then you're used to the climb," he said. "C'mon." To my relief, he turned and left the bridge and started down the extremely steep embankment toward the river. I scrambled along behind, annoyed by the fact that he'd worn a pair of rock-climbing boots while I had only my professorly penny loafers. We slid most of the way down, starting little rock-slides here and there, and ended up on our fannies several times before we reached the bottom. It was a wild-goose chase for me, but a grand adventure for him. He was jauntily resigned to the task, always the teacher, the patient, enthusiastic father figure who'd gladly take his adopted sons and daughters to the moon to further their knowledge.

* * *

"Slope's nothing," he said at the bottom as I stopped to empty the dirt from my hoses. "Mountains here are foothills compared with the Rockies." He moved off along the rock-strewn bank of the swollen river. "Show me where, lad," he called out.

"Around here. I don't remember exactly." I replaced my shoes and stumbled after him.

"River wasn't so high then, was it? Current wasn't so fast." He squinted at me and I wondered if he knew I was lying. Teachers have a way of knowing what their students are up to. He looked down at the thousands of loose, river-polished rocks at our feet. They'd all come from somewhere else: pieces of mountain broken off and rolled along in the water, piled up and patiently waiting for the next flood to move them. So many had already passed and so many more would come, and we could never pick through them all for that grain of salt we called a diamond. The Rock seemed to realize this as he looked down, and he took the easier course of describing the grand geology.

"This valley is deeper than it is wide," he said. "From the edge of the bridge, you can hit a three-wood across the expanse. I've brought classes out here and done it."

"It's too far. . . ." I looked up at the bridge, which appeared to be much longer than the four-hundred-foot depth of the gorge.

"Optical illusion, lad. A good three wood'll do over two hundred yards and land way up on the other side. Should have brought my clubs and put it into perspective for you."

For the first time, I thought there might have been a good reason for our astronauts to hit golf balls on the moon.

He continued to walk along the river bank. He knew where

to step and how to handle the rocks, while it was all I could do just to keep my balance.

"What does the depth of this valley in relation to its width tell you?" He stopped and let me catch up to him.

"It's very . . . new?" My foot slipped between two sharp rocks and I was stuck a moment, but he gave me a hand and I escaped unhurt.

"Brilliant. lad." he smiled while I checked to see that my sock hadn't ripped. "The Green River is just that. It cut this valley so recently that the sides haven't had time to wear down."

"So the diamond didn't come from this spot."

"Not a chance. It's traveled many miles, probably, and these mountains'll be worn flat before anyone finds another one here." He went along the riverbank ahead of me again, occasionally bending to chip at some rocks with his hammer. I stood and watched him a while, until he was a good distance away. He was going through the motions for me, I thought. He was probably bored with such a new river valley that he'd already visited so many times, and he should have been a little out of sorts to be on such a fool's errand, though he didn't show it. It felt guilty to have been so useless; not to have known where I supposedly found the stone and, worse, to have worn my stupid penny loafers. I wanted to kick around in the rocks with him, at least to make a show of it, but my feet were getting sore and cold. I wiggled my toes to warm them and then looked down and noticed that I'd stepped on an interesting stone. I stooped to inspect it and pried at it with my fingers, but it was lodged among some larger stones and would not come loose. I became so absorbed to the task of removing it that I did not hear The Rock approach behind me.

"Need this, lad?" His voice startled me, as did the mason's

hammer he dangled next to my ear. It was a sinister weapon. The blunt end could have easily caved in my head; the sharp, chisel-like side could have split my skull like a melon. The thing twisted on its rawhide loop, and cold steel brushed my ear. I flinched and looked up at The Rock, but his eyes were fixed on the stone I'd found. He flipped the hammer up and into his grasp, like a policeman with a nightstick, and squatted next to me. Then, with two short, deft swings on the chisel side he easily extracted the stone. "Good specimen," he said, "but only quartz." He wiped it on his pants and offered it to me but I shook my head. I did not want to touch it, nor did I want that hammer of his again to touch my ear. I kept my eyes on him as he stood and flipped the stone into the turbid river.

"That'll take it a few miles," he said, "and polish it a little better." He turned and ambled away, and chipped at some more rocks.

I touched my ear where that awful hammer had been. It had made it hot. I'd always hated that, since I was a kid, to have one ear get hot.

$\bigtriangledown$

Chapter 19

THE SUN SLIPPED BEHIND the mountains and the Green River gorge turned gray and cold. The Rock and I had found a few more interesting stones but nothing of value or worth taking back as a specimen, so we pitched them into the river. I wanted to leave before it got dark, but he was like a young boy who'd play baseball until he couldn't see, until his mother had to call him home for the night. When we finally scrambled up the embankment to the bridge, we were out of breath from the steepness of the climb, and the light was nearly gone.

"Great fun, lad," he said as we reached the top and stopped a moment to catch our breath.

"But no diamonds."

"Diamonds are just rocks. Special rocks, indeed, but there are so many other marvelous things going on out here."

The last sliver of light flickered and went out, and the Green River gorge was black. We headed for the car and I made sure that he and his hammer went first. I thanked him for the field trip, though, and was about to thank him for all the trips he'd taken us on as students, but he suddenly stopped short. In the darkness, I nearly ran into him.

"Car's gone," he whispered.

I squinted at the rise on which we'd parked it and saw there was no big Buick.

"Left the keys in it." He shoved his hands into his pockets and brought them out empty. He shook his head, and I followed him up the rise to the spot where the car had been.

"Do you think it was stolen?" I asked. I realized how foolish the question was and quickly added, "Someone could have moved it as a joke."

He ignored my comments and began to consider our next move. "There are two roads in and out of here, for equipment trucks," he said. "You take one out and I'll take the other."

"Why?"

"If someone moved it as a joke, as you said, it could be on either of the roads. When we reach the main road, we'll walk toward each other."

"And if one of us finds the car, he'll drive back in on the other road so we meet."

"Brilliant, lad." There was a note of sarcasm in his voice that would not have been there if I'd filled in the obvious blank of some geological concept. I'd never seen him upset before, not in class nor even on field trips when he had to deal with all the minor catastrophes involved in transporting thirty or forty students to some obscure site. I was upset too, but for a different reason. I simply didn't want to walk out through those deep, dark woods by myself.

I took the road we'd come in on. It was no more than a rutted, muddy cart path filled with puddles that I couldn't make out in the darkness. I felt my way along as the deep chill of night in the mountains set in, and I wished I were wrapped in the Buick's thick insulation, coasting my way down to Sutherland and the promise of a hot meal. Careful though I was, I soon stepped into a sizable rut and cursed as water poured into my shoes. It wouldn't happen to The

Rock in his waterproof boots, I thought. I felt worse than just wet. I felt unprepared.

I continued along the path, listening to the squish of water in my shoes. It sounded like the Buick's shock absorbers and it annoyed me; the wind seemed to stop so I could hear the squish all the better. As I trudged through the evening doldrums, the pause where day leaves off and night begins, I wanted to run back and follow The Rock up his path. I wanted him to lead the way in his seven-league boots and to clear all the obstacles with his magic hammer. He'd taught me so much about our planet, but now I simply wanted to know how to get past the ruts in that crummy little path in the dark. I sloshed along like some big reptile-creature, an alien without his spaceship, an ugly interloper in that insanely serene world. Though the car thieves, or the pranksters, were probably long gone, I worried about meeting them and quickened my pace. I was anxious to meet The Rock, so we could hitch a ride down to Sutherland where my feet could get dry and warm.

When I reached the main road, he wasn't there. His path was probably longer than mine, I thought, so I walked it along the main road. I expected to see some cars, but none passed. There were no lights or houses along that part of the road either so, except for fewer ruts and puddles, it was no better than the crummy little path through the woods. It looked as though no one ventured into that part of the mountains at night, and The Rock and I were in for a long siege.

Within a mile, I came upon the spot where he should have come out. Still no cars passed. I waited and looked into the pitch-dark woods, hoping to see him emerge at any moment. I took off my shoes and dumped out the water, and then wrung out my socks and stuffed them into the big side pockets of my jacket. I replaced my shoes and walked in circles and ran in place to keep warm. I did not want to go back into the woods unless I had to. It was too creepy in there and, if for some reason The Rock couldn't get out on his road and had gone back to mine, it would set us on a merry-go-round so we'd never find each other.

I don't know how long I waited before I began to worry that he was lost or hurt and boldly started back into the woods on the road that should have brought him out. It was as bad as the other, filled with deep ruts and puddles, and I groped and stumbled along. At any moment, I hoped to see the Buick's headlights bouncing toward me, to hear the toot of the horn and see The Rock's friendly smile as the electric window rolled down. Then my foot caught on something and I sprawled forward, landing prone in the pushup position in a large puddle. I'd escaped total immersion but the front of my shirt and pants were sopping wet. One of my loafers was gone. Luckily it hadn't landed in the puddle, and I felt around and found it. I was freezing and my imagination was wild. I feared that I'd tripped on The Rock, lying in a bludgeoned heap as Cowpens had behind Elmer's Tradewinds. But it was only a rock, and I patted the lump in my jacket, now under a cold damp sock, to make sure it was still there.

I put the loafer back on and continued toward the bridge. The wind picked up and bit at my chest, plastering the wet shirt there. I was miserable and as cold as I thought I could be, until I heard something that chilled me to the very bone. It was a shout from the direction of the bridge. I wouldn't call it a scream, or even a yell. It was just a long, protracted expression of mild surprise, yes, a shout, that faded into the distance as though someone were falling a long, long way. At first I thought of running back toward civilization, not to the scary, forlorn bridge and its gorge. But I ran toward the shout, heart a-flutter and feet moving as fast as my soggy loafers would allow. I tripped again and fell flat on my face, but this time there was no puddle. I scrambled up and ran on, ignoring my stinging hands and the cuts and bruises.

When I reached the clearing where we'd parked the car, I saw nothing but the menacing specter of the bridge. I stopped and listened, but heard only my heavy breath. I called out for The Rock. Nothing. Only the wind answered and bit at my chest. I walked carefully down the slope to the edge of the bridge, and called for The Rock again. Still nothing. The darkness had smothered all, except that great bridge that loomed before me like a battleship, or an evil destroyer. I sidled out onto it, aware that another slip would be worse than falling into a puddle. I clutched the guardrail with both hands and worked my way toward the center of the span. It was so dark that I could not see either end of the bridge, nor the opposite guardrail. Though my body shivered, my palms were sweaty as I peered down into the gorge. I could hear the river far below, but I only saw black. If someone had fallen from that point, the current would have swept him away. He could be in some other county by now, on the way to the river's egress at the ocean where he'd filter out into its slimy delta and eventually rot with the muck of the millennia. If he'd hit the embankment, though, only daylight would disclose it. I turned away from the gorge and called out again, softer this time, expecting no answer. When one came on the icy wind that swept across the expanse, I was both terrified and amazed at the familiar voice.

"He slipped." The sly, Portuguese intonation was unmistakable. I could not see him, but Carlos was out on the bridge with me.

"What are you doing here?" I wanted to know but, more immediately, I wanted to locate him by his voice.

"Looking for diamonds, like you," he said. The wind fooled me and his words seemed to come from three different directions.

"Where's Professor Hill?"

"I told you, man. He slipped." Finally I spotted him directly across the bridge from me, by the opposite guardrail.

"You mean he fell off the bridge?" My voice cracked.

"An accident, man." He used the same oily tone to pick up girls at El Cid.

"We've got to get help!"

"You kiddin'? That's a long drop." He moved toward me, out of the darkness, and his footsteps echoed on the cold concrete.

"At least we can go look for him."

"Forget it, man." He kept coming, and I could see that his right hand was extended, as though to shake hands. Then I realized he held a gun.

"What's with that?"

"Don't worry. You won't fall off the bridge. You've got something too valuable."

"How do you know . . ." I stopped myself, and resisted patting the lump in my jacket.

"I knew before you, man. The old geezer brought it to me at the shop. Wouldn't let me have it, though. He was a cagey old coot."

"So you killed him for it."

"No, man. And I didn't push the professor."

I was sure he'd killed Cowpens and The Rock, and that he'd kill me. My heart beat so fast that I forgot I was soaked and freezing.

"Give me the diamond." He moved in close and prodded me with the gun.

"Professor Hill didn't just slide off this bridge. And Cowpens Martin didn't bludgeon himself to death." I stood my ground. He shoved the pistol into my ribs, hard this time, but suddenly drew it back when we heard another voice.

"I personally dispatched that skody old redneck." Yates Sutherland appeared out of the darkness, holding up his heavy cane. "He tried to sell me the stone. I thought he had it on him, so I bashed in his cracker head. I am sorry about the professor, though. It's just that there's too many in on this thing now, and he had credibility."

"I don't?"

"You're a Yankee carpetbagger, from nowhere. If there's any accusations goin' 'round, you're the one who lived with that old bum, and you're the one who most likely stove in his head."

"Believe him, man. He owns everything down here." Carlos was right. One word from Yates and I'd go to jail for good.

"But I own the stone," I said. "At least, I'm the one who knows where it is." It was my only play, and I hoped they wouldn't search me.

They looked at each other, and Yates spoke first. "That confirms your guilt, boy. It's obvious you killed for it, and you might as well turn it over to me." He moved forward, cane held high. I stepped back until my butt hit the top of the guardrail, the only thing between me and The Rock's fate four hundred feet below.

"I don't have it." In desperation I held my palms up.

"You do, man. I know it."

"He's been watchin' you, boy."

"Did he watch me Saturday night, with Jody?" I stared at Carlos.

"I should kill you for that," he hissed and shoved the gun at me.

"Now, boys. That's somethin' y'all can resolve after I get the stone. Give it over."

"I don't have it. . . ."

"Give it, boy!" He raised the cane even higher.

"If you kill me, you'll never find it."

He stopped and thought a moment, while I kept my eyes on the ponderous cane.

"We can deal on that level," he said. "But, first, let's make certain you're tellin' the truth." He nodded for Carlos to search me.

"I'll save you the trouble," I said, and reached into the pocket of my jacket. Yates smiled and lowered the cane, and Carlos did a nervous little samba. They looked at each other as though they'd won, until I plucked the stone from my pocket and held it out over the guardrail.

"That'd be mighty foolish, boy."

"We won't hurt you, man."

"Give it over now, and you're home free." Yates's voice had turned into sweet molasses.

"I'm dead either way."

"Not at all. You're too good a teacher," he said absurdly. "I've heard good things about your classes."

"Professor Hill was ten times the teacher I am, and look what you did to him."

"I told you, boy, he had credibility. . . ."

I'll never know exactly why, but I let go of the stone. The earth stood still as a billion years of fiery creation slipped silently off into the night. The three of us froze and listened, as though for a scream or a splash. Even the wind stopped in awe. The diamond was gone for good, down the floodstage torrent of the Green River, to another county, to be deposited with The Rock in the muck of the millennia.

* * *

When the world started again, it was in slow motion. Yates swung his cane and I had time to duck. The heavy gold ball, which had eliminated Cowpens, merely brushed the top of my head. His follow-through extended out over the guardrail, and I used that split second to deliver a swift punch under his heart. It was so simple, so reflexive, like a crisp volley in tennis. And the blow, plus the momentum of his swing, launched him into a four-hundred-foot nosedive, accompanied by a screeching wail of terror.

"Shit!" Carlos continued to hold the gun on me, but there was panic in his voice.

"I didn't mean it," I said almost sheepishly.

"Shit, man. I don't believe it."

"What now?"

"I don't know." He threw up his hands in confusion, and then realized his mistake and quickly aimed the gun at me again.

"There's no more diamond," I said.

"No more Yates Sutherland, either."

"I said I didn't mean it."

"You killed him, man, not me."

"Self-defense."

"Sure . . . but who's gonna believe that?" As he spoke, and thought more about the situation, he calmed a little.

"What about Professor Hill? And Cowpens?" I asked.

"You heard Yates. He shoved the professor over when I was back in the woods hiding the car. Hey, I'm holding the gun. I'll ask the questions."

"Are you going to kill me?"

"I should . . . for Jody. . . ."

The moon had begun to rise, and for the first time I could

see Carlos's eyes. He looked past me, off the bridge and into the black gorge of the Green River valley.

"I wanted so much in this country," he said. "I thought Yates could give it to me. He loaned me money for the shop, got me a special lease, rich customers . . . I thought I had the world by the balls, man. Then this thing came along. This little old geezer with this big rock. Yates wanted it so fucking bad. He was so rich . . . but so fucking greedy. Sure, I wanted it too . . . but not enough to kill."

He was silent a moment, then he turned his gaze back to me and poked me with the gun barrel. It pushed my ice-cold shirt against my ribs and I shivered. I expected his hot temper to explode and send six bullets into my chest. Instead, a silly grin crossed his face and he poked me again. It tickled.

"I don't even want Jody that bad, man. Besides, she likes stale poetry, not rich jewelers. And I know she'll never change." He slowly lowered the gun and then tucked it away into his clothing.

"What about them?" I pointed down at the river.

"Two accidents." He shrugged.

"Did you come here with Yates?"

"Yes. In my car."

"Who else knows you're here?"

"Just you."

"It could work," I said. "We go back to Sutherland in your car, and when they find Professor Hill's car, and the bodies, they'll assume they came out here together and fell into the river and drowned. One things bothers me, though."

"I know, man. We could go to jail for a very long time."

"No. It's that they might think Yates jumped into the river to try to save Professor Hill."

$\triangledown$

Chapter 20

THEY FOUND YATES SUTHERLAND two miles downriver,
jammed among some rocks and badly mangled, but still
clutching his gold-headed cane. I needn't have worried about
him being made into a hero, though. No one would think
he'd jumped in to save The Rock carrying that heavy cane.
The newspapers stated only that he'd fallen into the river
and drowned, and none mentioned foul play.

They never found The Rock, and I figured that's the way he
would have liked it. Like most scientists, he was a romantic.
It would have appealed to him to slip off into the endless river
of time, to be eroded, transported, and then deposited throughout the unexplainable universe, to finally bow and blend in
with the unimaginably ponderous elements.

For the next few months, I expected to be confronted at
any moment by the detective in the brown suit. But he never
came. Many times I thought of going to him and disclosing
the whole story. But Yates had already paid dearly, and I
could only malign his name and the college, and probably
myself, so I kept silent.

I never saw Carlos again. We made that decision on the
ride down to Sutherland that night. It was safer that way if
there was an investigation, and it was safer for us because

of Jody. She pulled me through those months. Her erotic whispers in Latin and her sunny smile kept me going through the remainder of that semester and the next. She made me slow down and live with the South, where I'd so hastily blazed through my undergraduate days like Sherman marching through Georgia. Sometimes I'd stay at her apartment, when her roommate was away, and sometimes she'd sleep over with me at Mrs. Carswell's. Other tenants occupied Cowpens's and Warren's rooms, but I kept to myself when I wasn't with Jody.

$\triangledown$

Chapter 21

My wife called. I don't know how she found me, but she left her number at the college switchboard. The area code was for upstate New York and when I returned the call she wouldn't tell me exactly where she was or how she knew I had been teaching at Sutherland College. She did say she wanted me back, that she was finished with the horse trainer and regretted what she had done, and that our little girl was fine. Her voice sounded strange, an echo on the line, as if she were talking down a tube. She was so far away, in a place so cold. I felt sorry for her searching for me all over that distance, explaining to the Southern operators, their marshmallowed sweet-potato voices and all.

We resolved nothing. I couldn't know if it was love, passion, or conscience that had prompted her call. And though I'm forgiving by nature, I couldn't believe that she wouldn't leave me again. I could live without her, I was certain. But the one thing I'd have to come to terms with was our baby girl. I loved her dearly, and though I've tried to be matter-of-fact about our separation, her little finger smudges on the windshield of my Tempest can never be wiped from my memory. When my wife and I hung up the phone, my daughter was as lost to me as the Star of Sutherland. It doesn't seem to matter now if it was easy or hard to let go.

I left Sutherland when the college year was over, for another teaching job in another Southern state. Jody came with me.

If you enjoyed this book and would like to receive details of other Walker Mystery-Suspense novels. please write for your free subscription to:

Crime After Crime Newsletter
Walker and Company
720 Fifth Avenue
New York, NY 10010

All books—except those marked 7-day
books—may be retained 2 weeks, and
may be renewed once for 2 additional
weeks, if not on reserve. 7-day books
may be retained for 1 week, and may
be renewed for 1 additional week, if
not on reserve. 10
    A fine of 5 cents a day shall be paid
on all overdue books.
    Loss or damage to books must be
made good by the borrower, if the card
is to remain valid.